Faith of The Cosmos:
The Beginning

William Curl

A Green Oak Press Book

Faith of the Cosmos:

The Beginning

William Curl

© 2014 William Curl

GREEN
OAK
PRESS

Green Oak Press, LLC
P.O. Box 6756
Lawrence Township, NJ 08648

Production Managed by:

John J. Errigo, M.S., Ph.D.-c

Publisher

In Partnership with:

William Curl

Author

Print ISBN: 978-1-940927-05-3

eBook ISBN: 978-1-940927-03-9

First Print Edition

April 4, 2014

$14.99
ISBN 978-1-940927-05-3
51499>

9 781940 927053

Fiction/General

Contents

Library of Congress Cataloging-in-Publication Data

In progress.

Write to the publisher or author:

service@greenoakpress.com

Social Media

www.facebook.com/GoPress

Twitter: GreenOakPress

www.facebook.com/booksbywilliam

GreenOakPress.com

Special Thanks!

Ben Denzer, the talented, thoughtful, and diligent designer, who worked hard, created and designed such an amazing cover, Thank you!

Cover design

Ben Denzer
Bendenzer.com

AUTHORS DEDICATION

To my Children:

Italy Marie Curl and Easton David Curl

INTRODUCTION TO STORY ONE

*T*hroughout the writing of the following story, I was asked several

times the obvious question, "what is it about?" At first, I struggled for a proper response and would often times spew out, "well, there's a lot going on in it," in an attempt to avert the question a bit. "There's a little religion, a little science, and a little theory," I would respond. After all, the true inspiration for the story was simply an assignment for a college course I took at Mt. Hood Community College in the fall of 2013. I enrolled in a religion course as a way to fulfill an associate's degree because I needed an elective, and because it sparked an interest in me. The paper was essentially meant to be a research paper, in the form of a story, which was to be completed over the duration of the term. With that thought in mind, it is my most sincere belief that things happen for a reason.

Before that term, I applied to a highly competitive physical therapist assistant program at Mt. Hood Community College. I had a 4.0 grade point average and completed all of the requirements to apply for the program. I even felt very confident about the interview process, as I had been prepped beforehand by a couple of the career counselors, one of which was a former instructor of mine. Nevertheless, I didn't get in and wasn't planning on waiting an entire year to reapply. So, I switched gears so to speak, and began pursuing a plan B. I had developed a deep passion for anthropology and decided that this would be my next pursuit.

At this point I needed a few more classes, for the most part electives, to get an associate's of arts before I transferred back to a four-year university to finish up my bachelors in anthropology. As I mentioned, I came across a Religion 210 class, a survey of World Religions. Unbeknownst to me, this would lead to the beginning of one of my greatest creations, which I give to you now. To my instructor, Timothy Watson, I have to extend a very grateful, thank you, as he gave us all a template to use to complete the story. I obviously took advantage of the opportunity to expand on it a bit.

So back to the question, what is it about? Well, I now believe I have that answer. As a child, just as any other, I asked the same question every child contemplates; where do we come from? It's almost a two-part question however, and as we develop chronologically as well as intellectually, that question tends to produce the follow up, where are we going? These questions have been the source of many great mysteries. They seem to transcend the boundaries of many of the supposed "concrete notions" that we have developed; for even if you never waver from your science, or religion, with these questions, you are undoubtedly forced to perpetually reevaluate what your beliefs are. They are mind-opening questions that either reinforce your belief systems about our creation, or introduce you to new possibilities. Over time and with age though, many other real world questions tend to take precedence it seems, and somehow these basic to our nature, questions, get lost in the recesses of our reality. In my life however, the thirst for this knowledge only grew over time, and provided the basic elements necessary to nurture many different theories of my own, in the stream of my conscience.

My own personal journey for clues has led me to a firm belief system. It is my personal belief that everything in existence, in its truest sense, was spawned from the same genesis, the same creator. Essentially, everything in the universe is the composition of "star stuff," if you will. If we apply the theory of evolution on a cosmic scale, the one theory of humanity's own development that has so far, stood the test of time, then we can see and understand that everything, everything in existence has its origin from one source, and in that sense, we are all universally connected, and by all, I mean all of creation, everywhere.

Furthermore, I've come to the conclusion that our beginnings are no doubt from origins other than human. Many religions propose this revelation through the fact that our creators are of other worldly divinity, and possess supernatural qualities that we do not. You can find these themes in every major religion, and in many creation stories from different cultures on several continents.

In theory, many contemplate our beginnings to arise from these other worldly realms as well. One theory, ancient alien theory, strikes me as the most compelling evidence for our creation from a theoretical standpoint. It hypothesizes that, thousands of years ago, space travelers from other planets visited Earth, where they taught humans about technology and influenced ancient religions. As of this writing in the winter term of 2014 at Mt. Hood Community College, I am enrolled in a Biological Anthropology class. Again, my highly held belief that things happen for a reason has been reaffirmed, for in it I have been provided with a very clear and meaningful description of our beginnings from a scientific standpoint.

From the book, Biological Anthropology Seventh Edition, by Michael Alan Park, it states that, "Evolution and its application to the human species-how we descended from nonhuman ancestors, how we have changed over time into modern Homo sapiens, and how we are still changing-is a central theme of bio anthropology. The fact of evolution is well supported by scientific examination-the idea has passed every scientific test applied to it. Scientists, however, are still debating the details of evolution and refining the theory that explains how evolution operates. It took some time, though, for the scientific method to be applied to this idea."

It goes on to say that, of Darwin, who is credited for this theory, that, "Like any great scientific accomplishment, Darwin's was based on the work of many who came before him. He stood, as Isaac Newton said of himself, 'on the shoulders of giants.' Darwin's genius was in being able to take massive amounts of data and assorted existing ideas and, using an imagination possessed by few humans, put them all together into a logical, cohesive theory that made sense of the world and that could be examined by the methods of science."

The great significance of it all, and one thing that has become crystal clear to me is, weather we are believers in science, religion, or neither, the only explanations we can generate for our creation, and where we are going, revert back to this bold concept; we are of nonhuman origin, and this concept is supported by religion, science, and theory. Also, I have found that faith is the foundation of imagination, for it fuels imagination and allows it to become our reality. Imagination thus gives birth to science, for before we can test a hypothesis, it must first begin with a thought, with, imagination. Therefore, faith and science are one in the same, as these concepts are married by imagination and theory.

So, all in all, like Darwin, I have aimed to do a similar thing. I'd like to propose possibilities to the world. No, I don't have the answers, but I may be onto something indeed. The following story is essentially, a story about us. It is a fictional tale about Travis. Travis is thrown right into the raw concepts of creation, and is forced to consider his own position in it all. My hope is to encourage imagination, to help you foster a mindful and open approach to these questions, and to inspire you to formulate your own theories of everything, through imagination. With that thought in mind, it is my great pleasure to present to you, The Elucidation of Star Beings Part 1: Travis.

THE ELUCIDATION OF STAR BEINGS

PART 1: TRAVIS

CHAPTER 1

*I*t's been cold these days, colder than normal for this time of year. I guess it doesn't help when the electricity wasn't paid on time and the only blankets we get in our hall have covered more bodies than the NYPD blood splatter unit. That said, I guess there are upsides to being a ward of the state of New York. I never have to worry about a meal or a roof over my head, but I'm pretty sure some of the prisoners' upstate lives in more luxury then we do at times. Who cares? In another 3 weeks I'll have a lot more on my plate to worry about than if I'll have a bed, much less blankets. My birthday is in early January and I'll be 18; no longer the property of, well I guess I should say in the custody of, the state of New York. Property feels more like it, but like I said, who cares?

I've been a ward here ever since I can remember. Many have come and gone. Some were adopted. Some ran away. Some even died, ever since I can remember. That's the most troubling thing about this whole process to me lately. I can't seem to remember much before my 7th birthday here, a little over a decade ago. It just seems like my thoughts hit repeat and I can't recall anything before that day, the day I met Brian. That's what troubles me the most.

Most here like me, served their time. Then the day came where there number was called. "Join the ranks of the real world. This is what we've prepared you for. You are no longer the custody of the state of New York, but that doesn't mean you're alone. Just remember that." Those are Brian's favorite words; Brian's famous speech to each new group of independent "young adults" whose time has come to cast their lot and join society as respectable young American citizens. Coming from Brian it's actually believable, but from anyone else here, it may have well been read strait from a sheet of paper that holds about as much promise as a Get Out of Jail Free card at Rikers Island. That's what the counselors and officers here in the G ward of the south hall offer us day in and day out; absolutely nothing. Most are here to do a job and go home; make a paycheck so they too can survive and be respectable American citizen's themselves, secretly hoping that somehow we will fade away without a trace in the same numbers that we showed up. "Do the country a favor instead of adding to the problem," I can overhear them grumble in quiet, but not so discreet conversation. Brian however, Brian is different.

Well, not different in the sense that he stands out in any special way. He sticks out in crowd as much as Waldo. He's pretty clean cut. He kind of looks like Adam Sandler's older brother; just a regular guy, but he's different. He cares, and he doesn't have to. He just happens to be a reverend. Or is it a pastor? I don't know, he's a Christian, but I doubt that has much to do with his compassion for the youth of this ward. He's just that kind of guy; different from the rest of them here. He takes time to hang out with us, invest in us. He wants to be a friend to us when that's all most of us really want, someone to accept us, and Brian gives us that without expecting the best or anything else from us in return. "I am one of you guys. I grew up here. I was raised right here behind these faded blue walls. I too had many dreams of what it would be like to be on my own, to have a family; not to have to be confined. I dreamt for years of the time I'd be surrounded by people who loved me unconditionally. I too have wanted to feel what the holidays would be like with a family of my own. I know exactly what you're going through. I've been there." Those are the reasons he cares so much, not because something in a book told him he had to. I don't know, I guess I never really asked why he cares so much. I never had to.

He's different, but today he really is different. At least he's acting different. Something is up and I'm going to find out exactly what it is. After knowing Brian for the last 10 years, and practically being raised by him, I can read him like an editor for the Oxford English dictionary. Anything outside of his somewhat bland, happy go lucky demeanor and it's the next thing to 9/11 for him. He's one of those almost akin to a serial killer watching a horror movie; it just about takes an apocalypse to stir him up, but today isn't the same. Something is different. Lunchtime, that's when I'll catch him.

My bed sits next to a window overlooking the courtyard in the center of our building. It's not much of a view, but it's offered me plenty of dates with Ms. Daydream, many dates that I've ever so longed for being trapped behind the pale blue of my room for so many hours of the day. Even though my view is a little skewed by the immense thickness of the glass, ever so apparently designed to prohibit any thought of escape, the site of staring into her eyes is one of the most beautiful things I've ever seen. I wouldn't say I'm a religious person, but it's probably the closest thing I've realized to true serenity. Alone in my thoughts, I can be anything. I can express my thoughts without being frowned upon, get comfort in my hopes, be forgiven. I can dream, and have faith in something more than my reality. I love her, my window.

It's 1 o'clock now, and that means I better leave my mistress and apologize for standing her up until our next engagement. I have to catch Brian and there's no time for looking into her eyes any longer. I have to see what's going on, and by the time I get down to the cafeteria I'm sure Brian will be surrounded by a group of guys in a hearty conversation about how the Red Sox will never beat the Yankees, or perhaps how someone we all knew from our hall washed up under the Brooklyn Bridge with an unearthly amount of narcotics still fresh in their veins. "Just another we couldn't reach. They had it coming. You have to decide for yourself the way your destiny will play out. Just another one lost," are the usual remarks.

Wait a second, where is he? Okay, so he's not in his usual spot right across from where I usually sit at the closest table to the food line. That's odd. After a frantic examination of the cafeteria, I see him. He's at the furthest table from the door in the back of the cafeteria, and he's reading something. The most unusual thing is, he's by himself. On top of that, the lunchroom is abnormally quiet and I seem to be directly under an invisible spotlight. I can feel the gaze of questioning eyes under tightly squinted and confused eyelids, and I hear the mutter of conversation so serious I'd think I was in the middle of mass at the Holy Innocents Roman Catholic Church up the street. As I make my way toward Brian, the roar of the crowd grows to a normal tone.

The closer I get I notice he isn't reading anything; he's staring at the table with his hands folded. "What, are you avoiding me or something? You're not sitting at our table bro, what's up?" I ask, as I give him a playful swat on the back. He doesn't even look at me, and doesn't respond. I move around and notice he's as stark as a dove in a midday summer's sunlight. "Hey, are you okay Brian, you really don't look good?" I continue. He doesn't break his gaze so I try another approach. "So what are you bringing plague and pestilence to the earth or what, you look like the damn pale rider?" I say with a laugh. In the silence that follows, my smile slowly turns to a blank stare. This is more serious than I thought. I take a seat facing away from the table. I'm done speaking until he says something.

After what seemed a lifetime of staring at nothing in particular, I notice it's almost 1:45 and I haven't even seen what they are serving for lunch today. As I rise to get up I can hear the muffled sound of a voice, "I need to talk to you Travis, but I can't talk to you here." He still isn't looking at me, and my stomach feels like the truest form of tyranny for not feeding it since yesterday evening. "Well, let me grab some lunch and I'll meet you out," "At the coffee shop" he says, cutting me off; "10 minutes." He leaves still managing not to make eye contact. Something is very different today.

The smell of the coffee shop hits me with the swing of the door, and it's packed as always. Brian isn't here yet so I sit on one of the lounge chairs and start to eat my sloppy joe. It's no Ruth's Chris, but it's free. It's gone so fast I don't even realize what it tasted like. There's no time to savor the small details at the moment. I'm a little anxious about this whole exchange earlier between Brian and I, and now he's late. This is so out of character for Brian I now have a million different scenarios running around in my head like the Boston Marathon. As I feel a hand on my shoulder I hear Brian's voice, "let's go." "Okay Brian, I've been more than patient with you today, what the fuck is going on?" His facial expression doesn't even change in response to my fiery blurt, and he repeats, "let's go. "Let's walk and talk, I'll explain everything."

Brian walks out without even turning to see if I was following. As we exit he takes a right and still hasn't slowed his pace. I have to trot a little to catch up and I feel like I'm a speed walker pretty reminiscent to the old ladies in a Richard Simmons video at this point. "Slow down a little, what is going on?" I demand. He stops, and finally looks at me. "I'm sorry Travis. I know this probably seems really strange," he says, almost out of breath. "Are you okay?" I ask, "you're acting so weird today, what's up?"

After a short pause and a little time to catch his breath, he asks me, "Do you remember the day you met me Travis?" "Sure, of course," I assure him.

"What about anything before that," he follows up. "Can you remember your parents, or where you came from?" I pause, with the sudden realization that he may hold the answer to what I've been feeling the last few weeks, and he knows something, he knows something I don't. "You know I can't, don't you?" I ask, noticing that he looked away at the question. "Well I feel a lot better knowing that you know what I'm going through and that you have something to tell me. It's a little odd though that you'd bring this up all of the sudden, because all of this has happened to me pretty recently, and I haven't even told anybody about it," I say, attempting to immediately coax an answer out of him.

"Your name isn't really Travis," he tells me as he looks back up and into my eyes, "and you're much older than 18." "What are you talking about, so you knew my parents?" I respond with what feels like confusion and betrayal at the same time. He's withheld this secret from me for a little more than a decade. "Well, what's my name?" I ask. "It's not important," he says quickly, "what's important," "What's my name damn it?" I ask, cutting him off and starting to raise my voice a little. He looks around and back at me, "The night you came to me, to us, it was unusually cold for the time of year. We get cold winters around here, but this was a record low, kind of similar to the weather we've been having lately. I went out to get the paper and I noticed an enormous bright light, a fire in the sky the size of a small building, but there was no sound coming from it whatsoever, and it was close, within 3 or 400 yards or so. Even on this clear crisp night in the heart of Brooklyn, nobody else saw it but me. I looked around and people were going on about their business as if it didn't exist, and as baffled and in awe as I was at that moment, I chose to ignore it and started to head back in. Then everything around me turned pitch black, except for its light. It was the brightest light I've ever seen. Even facing away from it I had to squint and shield my eyes." He stopped and looked away again, then back into my eyes. "Look I haven't told anybody this in over 10 years because, well partly because I know how it sounds, I do, but I was also told not to, until the weather turned unusually cold, near your 18th birthday.

I felt a presence behind me, and without hearing any words, something told me to turn around, like it was speaking into my mind. As I slowly turned, the light faded and there they were. Three Greys, three fucking Greys. The Greys, you know the ones from every corny sci fi movie of the time, but there they were, right in front of me, two the size of maybe a couple of 2nd graders and one about half the size," he continued, "it was you." Trying to wrap my head around this and to figure out how to respond without hurting his feelings because I think he's actually gone insane, I feel like I've been the target of an eerie practical joke, but something deeper tells me I need to hear him out. He did know about my recent amnesia even though I never spoke of it. I'll hear him out, for a bit longer anyway.

"They showed me a symbol made of characters from your language," he went on. "It was your name. They fed me instructions; implanted them into my mind with a firm clarity as if they whispered into my conscious without ever speaking a word as you or I do. They said that the Greys are one of humanity's celestial ancestors. A large portion of the human species was created using a combination of their DNA with the DNA of an ancient earthly hominid, another ancestor of humans. They left your planet in search, in search of a better place for you, because they loved you. Your planet was literally destroying itself with wars, violence and carelessness. They wanted you to have a better place to call home, and they wanted you to one day return to your planet and bring back hope and guidance that could show the beings of your planet a better way of existence. Their hope was for you to bring religion to a place where religion was never realized. That's why I was chosen, and that is why you are here Travis. Travis, that's the name I gave you because the symbol kind of looked like it spelled the name Travis." The conversation went on for a little longer that evening, as he went into detail of my planet and my parents. The next step, he informed me, was for me to gather as much information as I could to make what he called, "an enlightened decision."

CHAPTER 2

*I*t's been exactly 2 months today since that conversation; a little over a

month that I've been gone from what's been my home since I can remember,

the ward. That conversation went on for what seemed like hours. I'm sure it

was closer to 30 minutes, but I don't think I said a word the whole time. I'm

still processing everything he told me. As he went on, the shock and awe

turned into a sick confusion, and then a realization that put together

questions I've always had like those pieces to a puzzle that looked as if they

came in the wrong box, and finally found a home.

Why couldn't I recall my childhood and recollect my parents in any

manner? Why didn't medication ever work on me, or more importantly, why

did I seem to never need it? My body has overcome any kind of sickness,

bacteria, virus or any other thing afflicting it since I was a kid, without the use

of drugs. Why did I always feel so different growing up, as I contemplated

the meaning of creation while my buddies were fighting or trying to have a

"quickie" with a hottie in the laundry room during one of the free times we

had to mingle with the girls in our building? Now I know the answers, most

of them anyway. In 3rd grade I drew a part of space that was a section of the

Eagle Eye Nebula. At that point in time, Hubble hadn't ventured to deep

space. I remember years later when the same image made it in a very

prominent magazine; Time, or Science, I don't remember. What I do

remember is the reaction I got from some of the faculty because those

pictures were hung in the computer lab we had in the H ward, with our

names on them. I was the true embodiment of a "freak," but it was my life,

and I thought it was normal, so these questions didn't manifest themselves until much later, until recently. That was the first time I'd seen Brian look concerned, but I wouldn't understand why until now.

That day, which seems so long ago, two months ago now, Brian answered many of the questions I struggled with, as if he stole my list for Santa Clause and read it to me aloud. He delivered it with a precision that took me through every emotion imaginable, however ultimately putting me in a state of comfort, much like a baby must feel when it's sung a lullaby from its mother. The funny thing is, even though he answered many of the lingering questions I've struggled with growing up, he left me with a new list of questions heftier than what I began with. That day, Brian shuttled me into this plan that was laid out for me over a decade ago; a plan that began centuries ago, with a thought by my parents that could change the outcome of a world. This is it, the beginning of my journey.

"Okay Travis, I haven't told Dinesh much about you at all, or the real reason we're here," Brian assured me as we walked into Radha Govinda Mandir Temple not far from the ward. "Isn't that against your religion?" I say jokingly with a nudge. With a smirk he looks at me and responds, "I said I didn't tell him. I didn't lie to him, right?" Brian has set up an "interview" as he explained it to Mr. Rangan. "Now remember," he says as stern as he can get, which is about as stern as the Charmin bear would get if he ran out of toilet paper to land on, "Dinesh is a good friend of mine. Oh, and call him Mr. Rangan." "No really?" I chime back sarcastically. "Come on, I learned my manners from the best right?"

An interview, I guess you could call it that; interview for what? "Interview, that was the best you could come up with?" I ask Brian as we walk down a short Hallway. "Just play along and I'm sure you'll get plenty out of him," he says as he stops and examines the walls. An interview; well, I do need answers, and Dinesh is "the best source of the Hindu religion in the five boroughs," according to Brian. Dinesh and Brian are good friends, and I was assured they've had many religious battles, verbally of course, over a cup of Brooklyn's finest; the coffee shop, host of some of the most intense holy wars known to New York City. As much as I joke with Brian, he knows how much I appreciate his going out of his way to point me in the right direction.

I'm still digesting the weight of the story he told me about myself, and I've second-guessed it as many times as the METS have had losing seasons. Regardless, I do want answers, and more than that, I've started to realize my own hunger for spirituality as I, grow up. If this all turns out to be just a crazy delusion of Brian's, and eventually fades with the coming years like my childhood memories, at least I'll get a blueprint of religion and what it means for so many others in the world. It's something I've never been introduced to before, or had the opportunity to explore. Anyhow, Brian knows, perhaps better than I do at this point, what exactly is at stake here and how important this information will be.

"Call me Dinesh," I hear off to my right. An East Indian man with really big eyes and a smile that appears never to alter its shape offers me his hand. As I shake his hand I notice how small he his. At the same time, for his age he could pass for one of my buddies back at the ward. If he's friends with Brian I automatically assume he's got to be in his late 40s, but he looks like he could have left the ward a couple months ago, in my class. "Dinesh," I say with a smile, as I make sure to give him a firm shake. "Travis," he responds. "Brian," He says with the same smile he had seconds earlier, "it's good to see you again my friend, as always." He looks back at me and says, "I've heard much about you Travis." It escapes from his lips so fast I have a hard time making out the full phrase. I made out enough however, to wonder what exactly he has heard about why I'm here, and I glance at Brian to see if his eyes will let me in on some of what he has shared, but as our eyes meet, he looks away. "Come this way," Dinesh orders as he turns and leads us up some stairs and out through a door to a deck overlooking Nevins street.

Moments later we are all seated at a small table containing what looks to be 3 cups of tea. "Please," says Dinesh as he gestures towards the tea. "Now Travis, I know this is very important for you, and me being a great friend of Brian's, I'm here to help as much as I possibly can," he says, speaking with a speed that could rival the fastest auctioneer east of the Mississippi. With that thought in mind, I wonder just how difficult it will be for me to grasp the depth of his words, but in the awkward silence, and stare from Dinesh with the same smile I met him with, I feel the weight of a much needed response growing every second. Interestingly, Brian hasn't said a word and is sipping his tea as he gazes at something very intriguing, which seems to be eluding the rest of us. He's told Dinesh more than he let on. "Yes," I respond. "Yes, thank you. I, um, we, Brian and I really would like to gain some insight on your beliefs; well, obviously more for me than Brian."

At that, Dinesh sits back in his chair, shoots a glance at Brian, and while still facing Brian rotates his eyes back at me and squints, without neglecting his smile of course. Brian is still in his imaginary staring contest with the people on the street. "I see," Dinesh says finally turning to me completely. "Well I would say Brian is pretty well versed in the beliefs of Hinduism after our many conversations, and I understand you are somewhat soul searching at the moment Travis. You are trying to grasp what spiritual path would best fit what you seek, correct?" he asks with great enthusiasm. "Sure, you could say that," I respond growing a little more confused as to what was discussed between the two of them previous to this, "interview." "Well Travis," he says getting comfortable. "Where would you like to begin?"

"I guess you could start by telling me," I pause in thought, "about, god." "About god?" he answers my question with a question, and a hearty laugh. "He wants to jump right in huh Brian?" he says appearing to snap Brian out of his daze. "Yeah, that's Travis," Brian says as if he joined the conversation not fully aware of what was actually said. "About god," he begins staring above him to recall what he's shared so many times, without losing his grin. "Hinduism teaches that God is an eternal force Travis. Some say it's an essence or power. Others say it's all of existence. This force is called Brahman. It is present everywhere, and in everything in nature. Ultimately, Brahman pervades everything in the universe and is also found within us. Therefore, the 'spirit' within us is Divine, it is part of God." "So are you saying that, we're, God?" I infer. "We're one in the same; all manifestations of Brahman," he follows. "Now, Brahman manifests itself in the material world in the form of physical beings that possess personality. This means that Brahman, God, can take the form of many gods and of many forms. Thus, Hindus may believe in an all-encompassing god or in a multitude of different personal gods."

"With that said Travis," Dinesh continues, "There are three supreme gods. One is Brahma, the creator. The other is Vishnu, the preserver, and then we have Siva, the destroyer. They each possess different realms of power and authority. "So Brahma is the creator, and what's the story behind how this world, I mean, our world, was created?" I inquire excitedly. My interest has seemed sparked. It's definitely new to me. "Great question Travis!" he says, raising his voice a little in his excitement. "Travis, many Hindu philosophies speak of creation, like life itself, as being cyclic. The Upanishads for instance, say the universe, Earth, humans and other creatures undergo repeated pralaya, or cycles of creation, and destruction, much as science speaks about the continuous death and birth of starts throughout the universe. Now, several myths exist that explain the specifics of the process. Nonetheless, the consensus view of the cosmos by Hindus is that it is eternal as well as cyclic." "Interesting," I say as I absorb this explanation. "What about Christianity Brian?" I ask more curious now that I've heard Dinesh introduce the topic.

"Well Travis, Christians believe that God created the world and all living things. He did this in 7 days, and in the Bible it says that man was created in God's image and given power over all living things. To me, this means that God intended humans to care for and look after the world." "This could also be a matter of interpretation," Dinesh adds, as the jousting seems to begin. "Many Christians believe that humans are the most important of God's creations, and some take this to mean that humans can use the world as they wish. To Hindus, because Brahman is everything, everything holds a similar amount of significance, which promotes respect for all of existence." "Interpretation is the key word here, and interpretation has been a tool by many who would choose to slander the word of the Lord, and to live as they please, by twisting the Bible into something it does not represent," Brian responds, with a stern grin of accomplishment, as if he's won round one.

"Now going back to our gods," Dinesh starts in, "we also have avatars, or incarnations of these gods." "That sounds kind of like Jesus," I say with a glance at Brian. I do know a little I guess. This blurt however, seems to light an imaginary fire under Brian as he contorts his face and becomes a light hue of amber. "Of course Christians," Brian cuts in rather abruptly, "Christians believe in the one, and only true God. God is the all-powerful and all-wise Creator of the universe. The benefit of us recognizing this one true, living God, is that because our God has real personal characteristics, we can have a loving, caring personal relationship with God. We can communicate with God. God speaks to us through the gospel and we speak to Him in prayer and worship. Furthermore Travis, man is not divine and cannot in any way become God. We are of course made in the image or likeness of God, but we are not divine and must not be worshiped. We also do not condone the worship of images or idols. This is strictly forbidden. You see, God is infinitely above us," he finishes, with his face engulfed in a tomato red. He looks a little uneasy; actually a lot uneasy, which isn't the normal even keel

Brian of the ward. Then again, I've never really witnessed Brian in a religious "discussion" before.

"Yes," Dinesh continues unfazed, "Jesus was an avatar; a great spiritual manifestation of God. Christianity and Hinduism are closer in ideology than Christians would usually like to admit. Christianity claims to be a monotheistic faith." "What does that mean?" I ask a little ashamed I don't know what he's referring to. "That means they claim to only have, as Brian stated, one true God. However, other major monotheistic religions such as Judaism, Islam, and Jehovah's Witnesses have somewhat of an issue when Christians make this claim. You see, one of the major things that makes Christianity an offshoot of the Abrahamic religions is the recognition of the Trinity. As an outsider to the religion like you and I, it appears that there are 3 distinct gods they worship and recognize." "As one," Brian cuts in more aggravated than before. "Wait guys, you have to remember, I'm a beginner," I quickly throw in, "what," "Let me explain Travis," Brian interrupts.

"The simple minded and those without faith like to simplify the trinity and take it as literal." "And why would you not take text for what it is?" Dinesh fires back. Brian, a little flustered continues, "Symbolism exists in every faith. We recognize God the Father, God the son manifested through Jesus Christ, and the Holy Spirit as completely united in will, goals, purpose, authority, influence and so forth. They are united in all aspects of creation and therefore, form one God. Does that make sense to you?" "Well, kind of," I agree to avert further argument, but I'm a little confused by the concept, "except, are they different beings, and why isn't there just one major religion? This is a lot to take in guys."

"Well Travis, you could say they are three different manifestations of the one true God," Brian affirms with an undertone of uncertainty. "So how is that different from what Hinduism says about Brahman," I ask. "I see," Brain says as he gathers his thoughts. After a short pause, he continues, "The

Father, Son, and Holy Spirit are in complete unity when it comes to dominion. Unlike the manifestations of the avatars in Hinduism, there is no contrast to one having dominion over say, fire, one over material things, one over creation and the other over preservation. We recognize this unity as them being as one. Does that help?" As I think of how to respond, Dinesh saves my wavering thoughts, "Perhaps these topics of Gods and creation can be visited again at a later time. I think as a beginner to any religion, a general concept or overview can serve more insight than getting too wrapped up in concepts. Let us, take a break."

"Excuse me guys," Brian says setting down his cup. "I have to hit the head; be right back." As soon as Brian is out of sight I hear, "Travis, why are you really here?" Dinesh is leaning forward and so close I can smell the tea on his breath through the opening of his smile. "What do you mean; I thought Brian told you why? I'm new out of the ward and just want some answers. I'm trying to, find myself, I guess," I try to convince him as well as myself. "Travis, I pay very, very close attention to detail," Dinesh exclaims. "I can tell you're a little on edge, and you suggested that you as well as Brian wanted more insight into my religion, which I know Brian does not need. When you asked about the creation stories of each religion, you asked how they explained the creation of "this world," instead of just simply stating our world, and then you corrected yourself. I found that a little odd. Now if you really want my help, I can help you the most if I know the true inspiration of your visit. I believe this is a little more than just an interview to you, am I right?" Just then Brian returns and upon his entry Dinesh picks up his tea and sits back comfortably, never breaking eye contact with me. "So gentlemen, where should we pick back up?" he asks, still staring into my eyes.

CHAPTER 3

"So," I say, trying to come up with a question but internally trying to

discern what exactly Dinesh knows, "What, what do you guys, what do you

guys believe in? "What do we believe in?" Brian answers with the same

question. "I mean, like, what are your main beliefs? What are, the rules, to

your religion?" "Would you like to start Brian?" asks Dinesh very quickly.

The beam of his stare keeps me frozen for a moment, but I finally shake him

off, and look at Brian. I'm not sure if Dinesh is still staring at me or not, but

Brian seizes the opportunity to take the floor, and I keep my focus on him.

"I can do that," Brian says, with his first smile of the afternoon. "Now I

think it's safe to say that, Dinesh and I can come to common ground on one

reality. I believe the main objective of any religion, at least our two, is for us

to attain happiness and the eventual fulfillment of our destiny, which is to

become one with god." "Yes my friend!" I hear Dinesh shout which

immediately snaps my focus back to him; he's averted his glance and is now

shifting his gaze between Brian and I. "Now how does that happen? How

do we go about this and what does it mean to be one with god? That is

where our faiths differ," Brian continues.

"Now in Christianity," Brian begins after a very brief pause, "contrary to

the beliefs in Hinduism, God will never be found within the heart of a

sinner," he says, shooting a glance right through an **X** on Dinesh's forehead.

With a roll of his eyes, and the same smile he's had since we met, Dinesh

sighs. "We are not just simply, part of God," He continues, "nor are we as

sinners, in fellowship with the Lord. No amount of works or meditating or

soul searching will make you one with the Son of Man. It's called Salvation

Travis. Our sins spiritually separate us from God and without forgiveness from God himself, no salvation can be attained, and if we do not attain salvation, we are cut off from the Lord." "What do you mean cut off from the Lord?" I ask. "Well, being cut off from the Lord would include living in sin, and ultimately, not achieving eternal life with God in Heaven," he says, squinting into my eyes to drill the message home. "So what you're saying is, we have to be forgiven, by God, otherwise, no Heaven?" I ask, trying to keep my response as simple as possible. "Sure," he assures, "you could put it that way." "So how are we forgiven?" I ask, as my intrigue continues to swell.

"He is the way, the truth, and the light. No one can come to the Father except through Him. "Him?" I interrupt. "Jesus," he responds as if he was waiting for the question. "There is no salvation whatsoever, apart from the sacrifice of Christ," he follows with authority. "Huh?" I impart, a little confused by the proclamation, "Sacrifice?" "The Bible explains that because of man's sinful nature, a divine sacrifice had to be made in order for us to be forgiven in the eyes of God," he follows. "In our terms the saying goes, 'you do the crime, you do the time;' same scenario here Travis," Brian says with a chuckle impressing himself. "Now because of God's loving grace he sent his only begotten son, in the form of man, to pay the penalty of man's sins. Through the death and resurrection of his son, Jesus, we can now be forgiven for our transgressions, and receive the gift of eternal life in Heaven," he says without continuing. As he waits, most likely for a sign of my acknowledgement, I quickly think of something to say. "So, because of that, that act, we are sin free and we can go to Heaven?"

"Absolutely not!" Brian retorts almost coming out of his seat. He sits back with a frown, I imagine coming to the understanding that he needs to treat me as a beginner. "You know Brian, this is the most animated I think I've ever seen you," I say trying to lighten things up. "The Bible says that to receive God's forgiveness is not without conditions on our behalf," he goes on with a scowl, and no recognition of the attempted joke. "In order to obtain the forgiveness that Jesus offers, we must believe in the Lord, and be willing to confess that faith. We also have to repent. That means we have to ask the Lord to forgive our sins. In the gospel of Mark, it is said that salvation is impossible apart from faith." After a pause, I inquire, "Have faith, and ask to be forgiven?" I'm sure he can see a hint of confusion on my face, because inside I'm extremely confused as to why such a powerful god wouldn't have the ability to forgive us if we asked, without such drastic measures as to send a form of himself to us to be sacrificed just so we can all be one big happy family in the end. Nonetheless, I leave that conversation for another day. Then I hear, "Correct," as Brian says finally relaxing the contortions of his face.

"Now there's more to the story. Of course the Lord will return, there will be a final judgment and so on and so forth," he says recounting this story somewhere up in the sky as if he's reading it from something hovering above us, "but I can see you're a little confused," he says looking back down and at me a little angrily. "No," I cut in, "well maybe a little," I admit. "So why don't we let Dinesh explain a little of his faith?" he says, beginning to regain his reddish glow. "Maybe his message will resonate a little more with you Travis. It does take a tremendous amount of faith, and understanding, and discipline," he continues as his eyes widen in sequence with his growing color, "to be a man of faith," he says as he turns to Dinesh.

"Transcending and liberation Travis," Dinesh begins, "these are at the core of Hinduism." "Transcending and liberation," I say, trying to show my acknowledgement and attention. "So for the Christians it's Salvation, and to the Hindus it's about transcending and liberation?" I add rhetorically. "Unlike Christianity," Dinesh continues with a piercing look in Brian's general vicinity, "Hindus believe that each atman, or soul which is part of Brahman, is free to explore its own path to what Christians would call salvation." "But to you it's liberation?" I add to impress upon him that I'm on board. "It's transcending, and liberation, and this can be accomplished by many means. Leaving this physical, material life, and traveling beyond it is what we mean when we say transcending. Any method, which assists one in attaining this goal, is called transcendental. Devotion and faith, austerity, works, yoga, selfless service, meditation, withdrawing from and deemphasizing attachment to worldly possessions so that material things lose their hold on your inner being, and knowledge of faith and ones divine place within Brahman; these are all means to liberating one from the hold of the cycle of reincarnation, and thus, transcending."

After witnessing through my eyes the assessing of this information going on in my mind, he breaks in, "Anyhow you see, no religion can possibly teach the only way to salvation above all others. Any path which is genuine to the soul is an acceptable means to liberation, and reflects the essence of Brahman. Each path is deserving of tolerance and understanding," he says with a proud and content tone, meeting the aggravated peer of Brian with the smile he's maintained today. At this, I notice Brian shift uncomfortably in his chair.

What I find amazing about all of this, aside from the interesting approaches each takes to stand for his religion, is the emotion and amount of tension that develops from them trying to take a stand for their faith. It seems that as human beings, as beings that have come from the same place and share the same origins, they would be more accepting of what each discerns as a holy way of life, but it almost seems to cause more division amongst them. Maybe that's one reason my people shunned religion. "Do you have any questions for me Travis?" I hear Dinesh say as he snaps me out of my thought. "You said something about the reincarnation cycle," I say trying to formulate the rest of my question. "Yes," he says assuredly. "What is that?" I follow. "Is that like when you're born over and over? I'm pretty sure I've heard of that, and would breaking that cycle be the same thing as going to Heaven to a Christian?" I ask more confidently with a complete question under my belt, actually two.

"Great questions Travis," he says in a whisper. "The expectation of Hindus is to escape material existence by overcoming the reincarnation cycle. Hindus believe that, when a person dies, his spirit is given another earthly body. This cycle of death and rebirth continues on and on until one is finally released, liberated you see? This cycle can occur hundreds, even thousands of times or more! Hindus believe that the soul reincarnates, evolving through many births until all karmas have been resolved, and liberation from the cycle of rebirth is attained. Not a single soul will be deprived of this destiny Travis, for it is the destiny of mankind." "Karma?" I cut in.

"There is no eternal hell, no damnation in Hinduism, and no intrinsic evil. We don't believe in a satanic force that opposes the will of God. However Travis, what is believed is that one's precise circumstances in life are completely determined by his previous conduct, either in this life or in the combination of previous lives. By doing good deeds in this life, therefore, one can improve his circumstances in the future, especially in future reincarnations. Essentially everything good or bad that happens to us in this life Travis, comes as a payment for this past conduct I speak of. Realize Travis, that nothing is ever the product of what others have done, but always the consequences or rewards of our own actions. This concept is widely believed in our own society today, by Hindus and others alike. To the Hindu, therefore, the grandest punishment of all consists of continuing to exist on earth. Does that help?" "Actually, yes" I assure him, "it makes a lot of sense Dinesh," and it did. The concept of Karma just seems like a natural one to me. "Great!" he says with an expansion of his grin. "So what was that though, about resolving all Karmas?" I ask for some further clarification.

"As I said before, leaving this physical life and traveling beyond it is what we mean when we say transcending. This is precisely what occurs when all

Karmas have been resolved Travis. All souls, without exception, will attain this highest spiritual summit, though it may take many, many lives, finally reaching the pinnacle of consciousness where man and God are forever one. So you see my friend," he says as he leans in, "this is the final goal of Hinduism, to escape or be released from the cycle of reincarnation. This Travis, is Liberation. I glance over at Brian and notice he too, is lost in a conversation; one existing only in his mind. Apparently he's left us to hash out the details, so I decide to inquire rather loudly, "I see, so is there some sort of place people go to learn about these things?" shuttling my voice at Brian with a slight increase in inflection. "Oh, huh? Well it seemed like you were very into Dinesh's, stories, uh, Travis. So, I thought I'd not interrupt for a bit. What was that?" he asks, trying to detach from the intense conversation he was having with himself.

"I asked," I begin, trying to reveal how unimpressed I was with him not being respectful to Dinesh, "if people went somewhere special to learn about these things, or if they're just expected to take it upon themselves to educate themselves on the subjects?" "Oh, well of course Travis," Brian says in an attempt to cover up his lack of attention while insinuating that this should be common knowledge for me. "What do you think this place is?" he asks with obvious sarcasm. Matching his sarcasm I respond, "a building, but no really, I mean I don't know if people just meet at these places to gain some sort of sense of community, or if this is where they learn how to practice their faith and worship, or what. I really don't."

"A very innocent question Travis," Dinesh steps in. With a glare at Dinesh as if Dinesh had just assaulted his big toe, Brian begins, "Most Christians attend worship services at church Travis, on Sundays. This generally includes song, prayer and what we call a sermon, or a message of the word. Are you with me so far?" he asks, attempting to ruffle my feathers and have me share in his irritation. "Got you," I respond with my own insincere smile. I make a mental note never to join Brian in a religious conversation again. I've never known Brian to have this kind of demeanor, and as practically a lifelong friend, I'd rather not let religion create any distance between he and I. "Most Christian churches have an ordained minister, or a designated person, to deliver this message to the congregation. At home, most practicing Christians pray regularly and many read the Bible as well." "Hmm, okay," I say with a nod to show I'm following, "and what about Hindus Dinesh, where do they pray, and worship and learn?" I proceed, trying to get more of a back and forth dialogue between the two of them.

"Well Travis," Dinesh starts in, "for us, Hindu's worship both at home and at temples. Our temples can be called just that, temples, or the more traditional name, mandirs. Each temple is dedicated to a god Travis. However, it is still the norm and permitted for people who worship different gods to pray at that particular temple. Many Hindu homes have a shrine, called a puja, where they perform ceremonies and worship. The images and idols of Hindu Gods and Goddesses can be found throughout many Hindu homes. Furthermore, we may not go to temple daily, but as a minimum, tend to worship at the shrine in our homes."

With a little bit of an awkward pause between the two of them, as if they're both rallying their wits for a second half, I take advantage of the opportunity to keep things rolling. "So what are some of the, I don't know what you'd call them really, practices, or rituals maybe that allow someone to develop their faith in each religion? Dinesh talked about it a little bit earlier, but I'm after a little more insight," I initiate, trying to express a little more authority in the conversation.

With a laugh, Dinesh, as I've come accustomed to from him, tries to lighten the mood with "he's a good pupil Brian! He's really becoming a student of faith; great pick!" Brian forces a half smile, which seems to be betrayed by the rest of his expression. "Rituals is a risky word Travis," Brian begins. "Risky, how?" I respond. "Well, a ritual is a more accurate word for pagan religions I'd say. They're almost better associated with magic and hocus pocus," he says, with a squint and a sneer toward Dinesh. "Christians would prefer our faith building methods to be called practices, or more specific, sacraments.

Many of our religious practices vary between denomination and church. Even so, there are very common practices to virtually all forms of Christianity." "Wait, so you guys believe in one god and have the same concepts of faith," I start in, feeling a growing pride of my developing understanding of these two religions, "but you have different practices from church to church? How is that different from Hinduism, where they have different ways to worship that result in the same end?" I ask, looking toward Dinesh for approval even though the question was for Brian. Though Dinesh's smile hasn't altered in the slightest, the face he presents looks to be one of confirmation. "Well that's a pretty simplified outlook on what I just said Travis," Brian replies in defense.

"There are slight variations in the interpretations on some forms of practice between denominations." "What's a denomination?" I ask unable to contain the question until he's finished his thought. "It's just a name for a specific Christian group Travis. Like Dinesh said earlier, just focus on what I'm saying and don't get too wrapped up in the details okay?" He says, unable to confine his impatience. "I'm just trying to learn as much as I can Brian," I say as equally defensive as he's been. "Would you like me to continue?" he says, becoming his familiar as of late, rosy tint that exposes him beginning to heat up. "That's what we're here for right?" I respond a little angrily. "Regardless of denomination, as I said before," he continues, "there are still many common practices amongst Christians. For instance, in general, our practices include things like baptism, bible Study, chaplains, showings of faith, The Eucharist or Communion, exorcism, fasting, acknowledgment of holidays, marriage, prayer, tithing and the list goes on," he finishes, with a glance at Dinesh signaling his resignation from this topic.

"Thank you Brian," Dinesh replies thoughtfully as he gets the signal. Before beginning he takes in a deep breath, as if to reflect this may be his favorite topic of religion. "Religious life of Hindus Travis, is focused on devotion to Brahman. This devotion can be represented in the worship of the manifestation of a god or gods, or through the perception of the essence of Brahman itself. This is the approach of many of the more philosophically minded Hindus, who seek enlightenment and liberation though intense mediation for instance. As I spoke of earlier, there are various approaches, or practices, regarded as equally valid. We can sum up these approaches under three paths, or margas, to liberation. Bhakti-marga is the path of devotion. Jnana-marga is the path of knowledge or philosophy, and Karma-marga is known as the path of works and action. With this in mind, it is important to realize that Hindu religious practices also center on the importance of fulfilling the duties associated with one's stage in life, as traditional Hindus are expected to pass through four stages, or ashramas, over the course of their life.

Brahmacharya, which takes place during the school years, is focused on acquiring knowledge and the development of character. Grihasthya, during what are called the middle years, is focused on worldly pursuits and pleasures such as marriage, building a family and the attainment of a career. Next Travis is Vanaprastha. This is a time when perhaps one's children reach adulthood, and is also a very important time of increased focus on spirituality. The fourth and final stage is Sannyasa, in the last remaining years of one's life. In this stage one may abandon the world entirely for a life of contemplation and preparation for what is to come. To address your question Travis, all stages of life for the Hindu nonetheless, involve specific religious rituals and practices, many times which corresponds to the stage of life one is in. I spoke of many of these practices earlier." "Well would you look at the time?" peeps Brian, surely at his boiling point.

At Brian's question, I immediately notice that Dinesh's smile has for the first time been overpowered by another emotion. Even though his smile still exists, I can't quite put a finger on the underlying communication of his eyes. It almost looks like he's in fear of something, or perhaps, intensely confused about what has just transpired. "Dinesh as always," Brian begins. "Now wait Brian, I think that out of respect for our guest maybe we should assure we have given him enough to go on; perhaps, offer him the chance at a final question," Dinesh cuts in, with an intense glaring gaze into my eyes trying to coax some sort of response out of me. What does he know?

Under a giant, invisible magnifying glass, I myself begin to feel a warmth as the pressure may detonate an explosive ending if I don't quickly respond myself. "Umm, well, umm; books," I say. "Is there anywhere I can get some more info or anything I can read to learn more about each of these religions?" With an oddly intense and irritated glance to each of side of himself, accompanied by a sigh, Brian says "The Bible Travis," and looks away from me immediately after. "No other religious guides are acceptable to God. The Bible contains the truth and the revelation of God's will for man; enough said," he finishes with a look now at Dinesh to denote the final passing of an invisible microphone.

With a somewhat disappointed look, possibly in my question and perhaps awaiting something better, Dinesh starts in with, "The highest written authorities in Hinduism are the Vedas Travis. These are the oldest scriptures in the world. The Brahmanas are authoritative commentaries on the basic Vedas. The Upanishads and Aranyakas are more recent writings and are authoritative as well. Lesser authorities would be the poems The Ramayana and The Mahabharata. The Mahabharata contains in it the Bhagavad Gita, which includes the very words of Krishna, the eighth incarnation of Lord

Vishnu. Most often these are not considered quite as high in authority as the Vedas, yet in practice they garner much greater popular influence," he says, with a slow transition of his eyes from me back to Brian, a nonverbal confirmation that he's wrapped it up. "Dinesh," Brian says as he stands, with an extension of his hand toward his old buddy, "you know how much I appreciate your time, and, you know how sensitive of a topic this could be for me." "My friend," Dinesh assures, "you are always welcome. Regardless of our walks, we will always remain one and share a bond in our stance of spirituality."

As the two shake, Brian looks at me as if to nudge me with his eyes, so I stand. After their embrace, he quickly leaves the balcony expecting me to follow. As I thank Dinesh and head for the door I feel a tug at my shirt. For the first time since I've met him, Dinesh's smile has dwindled to a strained grin, and he says in a quiet tone, "Travis, I know what it is you seek and I believe I know somebody who can help more than Brian or I alike. When the time is right, he'll contact you."

CHAPTER 4

I'm still not exactly sure what Dinesh meant by that last exchange, and I'm really curious what it is he thought he knew that I was seeking, because I'm still not even sure of what that is myself. It's been months since the conversation at the temple, and much to my surprise, I haven't heard from either Brian or Dinesh. I guess I shouldn't be too surprised though; I haven't really reached out to either of them since then either, so I guess we're even. Still, months later, the weight of what I've heard over the last few months still weighs heavily on my conscious. I've sort of reverted to my own best friend, and have been keeping my distance from everyone really. What surprises me though, is that even after Brian's proposal to "be there for us" once we were free from the ward, he hasn't reached out to me after that meeting with Dinesh. I don't know, maybe he's a little ashamed of how he acted. Maybe this was all just a big set up to initiate a wanting on my behalf to search for faith, and find some sort of spirituality in my life. Maybe it was his way of, "saving me," and ensuring he did his part to help another pagan child of the ward find the truth and the light. Maybe this really isn't fiction. I don't know.

In that time I have come across other Christians, and interestingly many have shared a similar aggression for achieving converts. It seems that every time they prove unsuccessful, it is followed by harsh judgment. "For none can enter the Kingdom of Heaven but through the Savior," or something along those lines I believe it goes. The problem I have with this is what about those millions of good, moral people who will never have the opportunity to ever hear "the word," say because of where they're from or because their culture belongs to another religion. Are they doomed to the same fate as the wicked and evil? Anyhow, I'm not one to stereotype. I guess you could say I just ask a lot of questions. I'm sure there's probably just as many loving and nonjudgmental Christians as there are the others.

I recently picked up a job at the coffee shop, and have a little studio apartment that I can barely afford not too far from the ward. I also enrolled at Kingsborough CC, which is in walking distance from my apartment. Other than trying to process my transition and all of this religion stuff, life has been pretty good. I'm not quite to the point where I'm ready to be out and about meeting people, but I still keep in touch with a few people from the ward here and there, on Facebook and through text. I guess it'll take time. Growing up as a ward of the state, I obviously never got the chance to experience this whole independence thing, and I guess I'm still learning how to be on my own. I have managed to get a gym membership with the little money that I have left over every month after bills, and I've been spending a lot of my free time there. I don't really know what the heck I'm doing in there, but again; I have a lot to learn. I'm realizing that the longer I live on my own the list of things to learn expands daily. Anyhow, I'm sure I'll start branching out here soon. I like the gym; maybe I'll start there. As I trip over someone's foot lost in my thoughts on my way back from wiping off a few tables I slip out a, "oh sorry about that, excuse me," and after catching my balance quickly look up and notice a man sitting alone at a table, not drinking coffee, not reading, just sitting.

"Have you been helped or anything?" I ask, flashing a smile that will convey my apology and customer service at the same time. He doesn't smile back, and doesn't respond. Something weird has just occurred to me in the split second after my question. I feel like I've seen this man before. "Hey, do you go to Slope Fitness off of 808 and Union St?" I ask, pointing over my shoulder in the direction it would be in. At that question, he slowly turns and looks into my eyes. The next thing I know, I'm coughing from the great cloud of smoke he's blown into my face. "Hey what the, you, you can't smoke in hear okay?" I say, starting to get a little angry. However my intrigue for who he is masks my anger at the moment.

As he conceals a pipe that I somehow missed before, the next thing that slips out as if it was a response mechanism is, "what was that shit anyway?" as I cough a little more. I'm pretty familiar with the smell of tobacco and even marijuana, but this was something else. As I gather myself, squinting a little to recover my senses from the intense smell, and still waiting for this jerk to respond, I finally hear "peyote, and no, I don't go to your gym. Sorry about the smoke," he says as he sits back comfortably in his chair ready and awaiting my next question as if I owe him an exchange. "Don't worry about it," I say. "So where do I know you from?"

"You don't," he reminds me. "Well you sure look familiar; you sure we've never met?" I inquire further. "We've never met, but I know you," he says with somewhat of a smirk that gives way to a more serious look. "You know me?" I say with a laugh and a little sarcastically, unable to hide my growing frustration with his indirection. After I repeat that, a realization slaps me into a slight shock as I am confronted with the notion that he's been coming here, and sitting in that exact spot for the last few shifts I've been at work. I guess I was just too busy to pay him any mind, but my subconscious somehow took note of his existence, and at this very moment one of the last things Dinesh said to me replays in my mind.

"You know what?" I say without a smile this time, "I'm not sure if Brian put you up to this, or if your buddy Dinesh conspired with the two of you loonies to try and fulfill some weird religious cult obligation or whatever the fuck is going on, but I'm really tired of the games. If they don't have the balls to tell me why they've done this to me and what their little plan is, then I don't want any part in it. So you can save yourself some time and effort. I'll be fine. I'm a big boy now and I'll figure out my life. The story was pretty interesting by the way, and you guys had me going I have to admit. Most people wouldn't go out of their ways to set aside that much time and effort and have such a well thought out approach, so yes, I bought into it; probably more out of appreciation that they cared so much for my survival and wellbeing, but you tell those two to get somebody else. I'm done! If you want some coffee or a pastry or whatever, I'll be behind that counter over there. Otherwise, don't waste your time, and don't fuck with me. I might look like a nice little guy, but don't piss me off!" With that I turn and head off.

"Travis, look at yourself!" he says so loud and with so much force that a few other people sitting by stop their conversations and stare at him. I turn and approach him, this time leaning in and nearly making contact with his forehead and mine. The smell of peyote is so intense I feel like I just took a hit. "Look, I warned you," I start. "Travis," he says without missing a beat, and with a stern controlled force, "Look at yourself." Confused, but somewhat entertained, I step back. "You're entertaining, I'll give you that," I say. "So what do you want?" "I want you to look at yourself," he says with a rising of his brows and a smile as if I was a little child that needed playful encouragement. With a laugh I come back with, "look at myself? You want me to look at myself?" I'm not sure why I did, but I looked down at my feet. I've done this at least a few times today, but something looks a little different. For some reason my pants are very frayed at the bottom, and now that I'm focused on them they feel a little baggy. Is this what he was talking about, and why would that be important? I don't let him onto the fact that I notice that, and I look up and say, "Okay?" He waits for me to continue. "So?" I ask with a pause. "What am I supposed to be looking at here?"

"You haven't noticed anything different lately?" he asks with a puzzled look. "Aside from the fact that I've got these new guns here, not really," I say jokingly as I perform a front double biceps pose. In the process, I get a little startled when I realize that the sleeves of my shirt are now halfway down my forearms. I purposely bought them a little tighter, and shorter in the sleeves to make myself at least feel like I've been making a little progress in the gym, so this is odd. For some reason, as I lower my arms I wiggle my toes and notice my shoes are a lot looser than they've ever been.

All of the sudden I start to feel sweaty and a little nauseous, and I intake a deep breath to fend off the lightheaded feeling that just crept upon me. He must notice these symptoms revealing themselves through my face. He leans forward quickly, "you don't look so good. Are you okay?" Feeling a little disoriented at the sudden recognition that, I must be losing weight, and fast; and, shrinking or something, the only thing that comes to mind is, "what's happening to me?" I take a seat across from him, and as soon as I do I hear "Travis, what are you doing bro?" My boss is now screaming at me from behind the counter. "This is rush hour in coffee land and you want to chat?" Hey, I'm talking to you! I'm not paying you to chat okay? Let's go, I need you back here. Tell your little friend he can chat with you when he buys some coffee, and after you're shift is over. Can I get you anything sir?" He yells towards, well I don't know his name, the stranger.

"It's okay Travis," he says to me. "I can come back when you're off. Listen, I know what's going on with you and you don't have much time." "I don't feel good Mr. Giovani. I'm taking off," I yell back to my boss. "Taking off?" he repeats. "If you leave don't come back Travis. This is your last chance bro; your last chance!" I lean into the palm of my hand trying to reorient myself. I do need this job. I need to regroup, and quick. "Can you come back later?" I ask this stranger. "I'm off at seven." "I'll be at this table," he promises. I almost don't even recall the rest of the day, and now, it's 7:10. My boss has gone home and I clock off, and gather my things. When I come out of the back, there he is.

"Do you want anything?" I ask, still unusually dazed as I approach the table. "I don't drink coffee," he says, without thanking me for the offer. "Well okay, so spill it," I say as I take a seat. "My name is Alo," he begins. "Okay Alo, no last name?" I respond. "Just Alo," he immediately replies. "It means spiritual guide in Hopi." "Hopi?" I ask, feeling like I should know what he is referring to. "Native," he responds sternly. "Oh okay, sorry," I follow genuinely. "You know I kind of wondered what you were, I mean like your race. You almost look a little Hispanic, but then again, maybe a little Asian of some sort; or both." At this he stares at me blankly, unentertained, and continues, "I was given that name because my parents were told I would be a special child; someone who could communicate with the spirit world. Naturally they expected me to be able to see the spirits of fallen ancestors, and to be able to communicate with them. However, it was never the spirits of the dead that came to me. It was star beings. All the same they were spirits to us; not of human form, but they came from the stars, and I began to be drawn to those of them that walk among us. I gravitate more strongly toward those that have more of an important journey to be fulfilled. That is why I am here with you now. "Well, well, Alo, you know what, it's fine? I haven't heard a good story in a long time, and I guess I should've expected this from those two since I haven't heard from them in months. I'm free the rest of the night," I say with a mocking intent. His eyes begin to pierce me as though some kind of emergency is in our midst.

"Reverting," he says unflinchingly. "Reverting?" I repeat, trying to follow. "When your race needs you the most, you will return to the form of your people. You are now in the wake of that process." Instantly that feeling that I had returns and my stomach tightens like I've just been kicked in the balls by an angry street peddler for not paying up. "Your clothes," he says, beginning to contort his face into a more serious gaze. "Your hair," he continues, as he examines my scalp with his eyes. As I look at my reflection in the window I notice that it has thinned to a fine straw look from the thick mane I used to possess. How in the world have I not noticed any of this before? "As I said to you before, you're running out of time," he confirms. "In our tradition, we pass down information through story. Let me begin with a story, first sharing my culture, and my religion. It will give you a foundation to understand the next part of the story, which will be to deliver you on your path, and the only weapon I have to assist you with is the story of our creation, and of the creation of religion itself.

Armed with this knowledge, you can return to your world a savior. For you see, the creators or your race and mine, even they themselves have gods of their own. As you have come to realize, religion takes on many differing roles in the same manner as cultures form contrastingly around our world. However, as we are bound by our DNA, in a common bond regardless of our culture, the philosophies behind any religion possess roots that bear the same fruit; fruit, which we reap in the end, to fill the same hunger that afflicts any race. In my journeys with religious leaders and through my experiences with star beings, I've come to the realization that ultimately the true essence of spirituality lies rooted in a common goal to establish a basic and true happiness for all of existence. You have the opportunity to share this ambition with the inhabitants of your world; however, time is not on your side!"

CHAPTER 5

*F*or the first time in my life, I let the possibility of imagination rule my

psyche. The unquestionable exposure to this new turn of events has left me

no choice. I've opened myself to the possibilities, out of desperation to come

to some sort of closure with all of this, but also because my curiosity for this

knowledge has seemed to almost form an existence of its own, and is growing

every day, intent on overtaking my reality. This must be what faith feels like.

"Native American religions are very closely tied to the land in which we

settle, but equally in relation to the realm of the supernatural," he begins. He

speaks with a slow and easy comfort; one that is seasoned through many years

playing the narrator during hours upon hours of lore. It's almost as if I'm

watching a movie and as I'm drawn in even at the first sentence of his story, I

slowly become less adherent to the surroundings of the coffee shop. I

immediately think, here's one time I'm actually glad this place is open 24

hours.

"As great as the number of tribes in the lands stretching from the red

wood forests to the gulf stream waters, so too are the religious practices of

Native people. Most tribes are aware of the omnipresent, universal force that

constructs all of existence. This force is governor of the three crises of life

which are birth, puberty and death." "You know," I cut in, "when I spoke

with Dinesh, he was saying a lot of similar things about Hinduism. I mean,

they're pretty similar because they also have many different avenues of

religious practice and highlight specific stages that are recognized as natural

progressions of our existence."

Hearing that come out of my mouth hit me with an enlightenment that these messages are actually sinking in; at least my interpretations of them. A slight pride creeps upon me and as I look at him for a sign of recognition, I realize he may be a little agitated that I jumped in on his story, and he doesn't in the least bit look impressed, but he does give me a nod and with it I reply as I break eye contact, "yeah, it is pretty interesting though." After a brief pause, he continues.

"Most tribes also recognize the spirit world to be of great importance, just as the world we occupy, and medicine people and communal ceremony are simply part of existence. However, many outsiders to our culture refer to this existence as religion. Native American spiritualties are part of our everyday lives. They are often characterized by the terms animism or panentheism. "Woah, woah, woah, you have to remember here Alto," I start back in, "Alo," he comfortably corrects me, "I'm a beginner with all of this stuff okay? What in the world does anim," "animism," he finishes my sentence as he looks through me, anticipating my next question.

"Pan-en-theism," he continues, more slowly so I catch the pronunciation. "Our animistic beliefs allow us the realization that all of creation possesses a soul." "So you guys believe that all living things, no matter where they come from," "all of creation," he stops me, "plants, what many would recognize as inanimate objects, natural phenomena; all of creation," he says with a still look and a certainty that paints this reality into my realm of possibilities. "Panentheism," he goes on, "represents that God and the world are inter-related, but not the same. So, we avoid isolating god from the world as traditional theism often does, while at the same time understand that there is a difference between god and the world and do not identify god with the world in the same fashion as say, Dinesh would.

Spirituality is as much a part of our everyday lives as would be working, going to school, even breathing. The natural and spiritual worlds have a deep connection within our culture. We understand that spiritual power exists in our people as it does within anything in existence, and through religious ceremonies, we are able to harness the aid of powerful supernatural forces to serve our interests." "Wait a second, Alo, you're kind of losing me here a little," I say with all honest intent. "So what you're saying is, you guys don't really have churches, or temples, or books or things like that? There's not really one, organized religion within the different tribes, right? Also you know Alo, you guys sound a little like wizards or something," I continue with a laugh, trying to gauge his sense of humor a little. He looks at me with a confused gaze, or one of disgust. I can't really tell.

Reflecting quickly on my attempted joke, the conversation with Brian and Dinesh replay in my mind, and I recount how sensitive Brian seemed to get about the confusion I expressed with his religion. I'm beginning to pick up that when discussing religion, as with politics or other hot topics, people easily become defensive and combative. It makes me wonder again if religion itself may be a tool of conflict, thrown at humanity by these, gods, to further divide humanity, or, there simply is just a common theme of ignorance among people that theirs can be the only true "way." Is this the true motivation of these misinterpretations of disrespect that seem to occur so frequently within the topic of religion?

Anyway, I notice he continues in full stride, "Native American religion tends not to be institutionalized. Rather, there is much experimentation and personal journeying if you will. At the same time, many aspects of our spirituality are very communal. Much of our spirituality is carried out first in a family or tribal location, and then extends into personal discovery. It could almost be better explained as a process or a journey, as opposed to a religion. It is a relationship experienced between the individual and the creator. For our relationship with God is experienced as a relationship with all of creation.

Creation is ever present and does not require an institution or building, or a book." "Okay, I see," I assure him, still internally attempting to make sense of his explanation. He gets a little jumpy at my acknowledgment, as if, losing himself in his story, he wasn't expecting my verbal input. "Journey," I repeat in contemplation after a short pause. "Relationship experienced between the individual, and the creator," I say to no one in particular, but aloud so that he knows I'm at least attempting to process what he's told me so far. I do have a question however. "So far, every religion has expressed it's own interpretation of this, creator," I continue on. "Who, or what, is it to your people?"

"The creator of all of existence is The Great Spirit," he responds, I can tell settling himself once again for an attempt at a winded narrative. It is called Wakan Tanka among the Sioux, and Gitche Manitou in Algonquian. Among some Native American and First Nations cultures it is a conception of a supreme being. To many of our people it is commonly known as either The Great Spirit, or The Great Mystery. The Great Spirit is personal and close to the people. One of the great spiritual leaders of my people, the Hopi Nation, describes the Great Spirit as all-powerful. It teaches us how to live, how to worship, and how to prosper. It shared with us a set of sacred stone tablets into which it breathed all teachings in order to safeguard its land and the lives of those that occupy it. In these stone tablets were inscribed instructions, prophecies and warnings. "So that's your book?" I ask enthusiastically with a slight sense of accomplishment.

"There exists no manuscript, mass produced with this information for the intent of study or the conversion of others," he replies with a slight scowl at my interruption. "It is sacred to us," he goes on, "and the knowledge of it has been passed down through the ages by our ancestors," he says matter of factly, successfully turning my perceived accomplishment into a dwindling flicker of an idea with no survival to keep burning. "Old Man is how the

Great Spirit is known to the Blackfoot people," he continues, not in the slightest bit concerned of my comprehension thus far or not, "and as knowledge has it within their tribe, Old Man personally created all things and personally instructed the Blackfoot people on how to attain spiritual wisdom in ever day life." "What about other tribes? Do you know how he, or it, is known to them?" I inquire as my intrigue becomes fueled with many ideas set ablaze by his words.

He displays a blank stare, which turns into one of intense contemplation. I can't tell if he's not used to this back and forth I throw at him during his, storytelling, or if he's simply recalling many stories he's told to others and gathering his thoughts. "Ababinili," he begins, "is how the Great Spirit is known to the Great Nation of the Chickasaw. In their tradition, Ababinili personally created all things and instructed the Chickasaw in matters of how to live long, healthy and productive lives. Ababinili is a very personal force to the Chickasaw. It is known to them that Ababinili has extensive communications with various parts of creation regarding the relation of mankind to other creation, and how this creation and mankind each ought to behave and co-exist." With a brief reading of my face and assessing my understanding, he tilts his face to the opposite direction during his examination, and continues before I can blurt another response.

"To my people, The Great Spirit is called Spider Grandmother. She is the force that created the four colors of mankind. However, she gave to the Sun the power of creation over all things and the origin of all spiritual wisdom. This is why to us, the Sun is the living manifestation of The Great Spirit, to whom we refer to as Sotuknang." He reaches for his pipe, looks around, takes a puff, then conceals the pipe under his jacket. He takes in a deep and hearty breath, closing his eyes and then looking straight into mine in preparation to further delve into the topic.

"The Sun has guided my people since the dawn of our creation. Interdependence and relationships between the real physical Sun and all of creation is acknowledged by my people. To us, it is not the same as the symbolism prevalent in the Middle Eastern or African religions, it is reality. In our culture, life is a process of change. This concept of change is of such great importance that a person is acknowledged as a new identity each day!" He announces with great pride. "With this understanding of the powerful dynamic nature of human identity passed onto us from Sotuknang, there is no need to create such static and speculative religious concepts as an eternal, final destination." With this he reveals an empowered expression and pauses to let this message set in. "That's fascinating!" I say, as I took his pause for an opportunity to pitch in my two cents. Then of course, another question sprouts in the water of new insights he provides my thirsty conscience. "So, does the Great Spirit ever, visit, or manifest itself to your people?"

Apparently, or I guess I should say, possibly, impressed with my question, he gives me an encouraging nod before he continues. "You see, The Great Spirit is not an anthropomorphic deity." His eyes begin to glow and he gives a slight turn of his head as he anticipates another question from me, so he quickly adds, "we don't give it human characteristics as other religions tend to do with their gods." At this, he appears a little relieved that I remain a listener, and continues, "The Great Spirit is similarly not anthropopathic." Again, he hesitates a little expecting a question, but to avoid my interruption, quickly goes on, "Unlike what say, Christians have done with their god, we don't attribute human emotions to something that is simply not human. Furthermore, The Great Spirit is not a panentheistic deity, as Hindus would say of Brahmanism, of which to them all of creation has stemmed and is encompassed and connected with. Rather, The Great Spirit is simply acknowledged to exist, possessing the power to guide individuals and communities. There are many tales of The Great Spirit's influence in our daily lives, however rather than being enshrined in a ritualistic, symbolic or codified religion, the tales exist as teachings we can interpret and apply to our lives on a moment-by-moment basis. You see, The Great Spirit does not represent a set of laws or codes to live by. The Great Spirit represents our culture and is ever-present in the daily needs of the nations.

So, as you can see, there is no one universal religion amongst the nations. However, each tribe does identify with the Great Spirit in one-way or another. As separate nations, we ascribe to our individual rituals, practices and ways of worship. Now, going back to your question earlier as far as books, there are sacred books that some tribes refer to." At this, he sits back in reflection and makes himself a little more comfortable. Again, I can't tell if he is offering me a chance to participate in the conversation, or if he's bracing himself for a second wind before he commences. I do notice that he has slipped his hand back into the breast pocket of his jacket where he's concealed his pipe. I reach out as if my hand is a powerful weapon capable of controlling all in its vicinity. "I wouldn't do that," I say, pointing over his left shoulder with my eyes. "New York's finest," I add as I notice an appreciative grin begin to form on his face.

Expecting a thank you, I hear, "Peyote," as his smile widens with a squint of his eyes. As his smile grows, I can't help but feel mine diminish, and I'm sure the confusion I feel is spelled all over my face. "The Native American Church is the most widespread religion indigenous to our lands. The movement started in the 1880s and by 1918 was formally incorporated in Oklahoma. We practice peyotism, and many refer to our religion simply as peyote religion." "We, as in, you, are part of it?" I ask, still not able to wipe my face clean of the confused look I had a few seconds ago. "Correct," he replies as he sharpens his gaze. "Peyotism involves sacramental use of peyote," he says as I see his hand fumbling under his jacket.

"Just as other beliefs among our people, peyotist beliefs vary from tribe to tribe," he continues without revealing his hand. Some believe Mescalito to be peyote personified as a god. Belief in the Bible is common, and Jesus is often viewed as a spiritual guardian, or an intercessor for man. The Great Spirit is also acknowledged in the Church." He glances over his shoulder in the officer's direction, and then back at me.

"In 1976," he continues, "the founder of the Native American Church of New York, Alan Birnbaum, petitioned the Drug Enforcement Agency to allow peyote use in religious ceremonies. His petition was met with great opposition and ultimately denied, so Birnbaum decided to sue. His stance was that this denial violated the First Amendment right to freedom of religion. He argued that when peyote use was banned in the Controlled Substances Act of 1965, exemption was provided for its use within the Native American Church." Again, he glances back, this time holding his gaze toward them a little longer, and revealing his hand a little further, then back to me. "In this case as well," he went on, "The Supreme Court decided in favor of the Native American Church of New York, announcing that it would be protected under the Controlled Substances Act. "Umm, so you're saying," I pause and look over in their direction, "you're okay to do that?"

"Traditionally," he starts back in, "peyote is used in pursuit of religious ceremonies. Understand, rituals can be conducted by oneself and with the creator, with a guide, a group, at any place, or anytime the creator and the participant deem necessary." As he reveals his pipe my heart begins to thump so hard I feel like if he was a little closer he'd see it. I'm not sure if any of that was true, or if those officers would even care, but I just wait in anticipation, and hope I won't be connected by association or whatever they like to say. He takes a hearty puff, and blows to the sky. The officers, lost in a hilarious looking conversation pay him no mind, and now I can inhale a little more normally as he puts his pipe back in its home. "The peyote ritual allows communion with the spirit world. It gives power, guidance and healing," he says as he slowly looks back down and at me. "This healing may be emotional, physical, or both."

"Wait, I thought you said your people didn't have an organized religion!" I say in response to the first thing that pops into my mind, "and why in the world would you combine Christian elements into your faith?" I go on. "Oh, and why, "First off," he says with a gentle force that stops me in my tracks, "I said our spirituality tends not to be institutionalized, but I was not done with my story before I was, interrupted by your, curiosity," he says with a scowl convincing enough to give me the sense he's not fond of questions. It seems to me he's more accustomed to storytelling, as opposed to having a dialogue. "Too many questions is like stealing thunder," he says. "Thunder was made by the gods to wake us up, to enlighten us to the reality of the upcoming storm within our midst. Now storms you see are rarely bad, and very necessary, as they maintain the balance of the world and fulfill what is much needed. So, let us not miss the influence of the thunder I possess. Tame the mind and be open to the essence of the storm. I've come to wake you. Now where was I?" he asks himself.

CHAPTER 6

*"F*or centuries," he begins, "man has made the ignorant mistake of

believing that we were the center of the universe; the most prized creation of

the gods. Through the ages the actual account of our creation has been

tainted by man's deceit and manipulation. The true story of our beginnings

has its birth in the stars. Everything that exists on our planet today has

origins from other areas of the multiverse. Our makers and their creators

have traveled from solar system to solar system, universe to universe, in order

to preserve the existence of several intelligent beings, including your race and

mine. Others call the stories that my people contain of these travels folklore,

or mythology. We call them the history of mankind.

Since the dawn of human race, from Tierra Del Fuego up through the

American Southwest and on to the Great White North of Canada, my people

have passed down this knowledge through oral legends and tales. The beings

we speak of in this history, some of us refer to as star beings, others as sky

gods. Many petroglyphs of these beings still exist within our lands today."

He pauses to read my comprehension, and possibly to assess my acceptance

of what he is telling me. At his request I hold back any questions that seem

to be accumulating. Come to think of it, I really don't have any at this point.

My curiosity of his upcoming story has overtaken any urge to include my

input, and I patiently wait for him to continue.

"Thunderbirds," he continues, "is how some tribes have referred to

them. In Iroquois legend, Hino is the thunder god and guardian of the skies.

The invisible spirit Keneun, another of the Iroquois sky gods, is chief god of the Thunderbirds. When he approaches, thunder is the sound of his beating wings and lightening his flashing eyes." With this, his eyes come to life. "Many tribes have stories and histories concerning the accounts of these beings and their relationship with our people. In most cases, these powerful beings act as teachers. They also serve as guardians and law enforcers, and most always they convey the importance of balance in all of creation." He pauses to grab hold of my eyes with his, and to make sure he has a tight grip. "I'd like to share with you some of these histories. You see, this is more than just a story.

As your guide, my aim is to give you a foundation; to offer you examples of what kind of impact you can achieve on your world upon your return. Chances are that upon your arrival, you yourself will be a sky god to them, and you will have the great opportunity of providing necessary insight, guiding them, and teaching them. You can bring to them hope and happiness. You can bring to them, religion. " As the words leave his lips my openness to receive his message has set in, and with it, an awakening of what a vast responsibility I have been entrusted with has embedded itself in my imagination, and has sparked an endless multitude of possibilities in my mind. If this is all true anyway, the next question would be, why me?

In recognition of this internal struggle that somehow he has caught hold of, he cracks a slight grin and makes his first attempt at lightening things up this evening, "you look a little tired Travis, I think you may need a coffee huh?" "No, no, no, no," I wave off his proposition. "I'm just, listening. I, I really am intrigued, and hey, I'm trying not to miss the storm, right?" I say as I force a smile through the deep contemplation and processing occurring as I speak. "Besides, I've been having way too much caffeine lately. I need to lay off," I add. With a chuckle he gives me a gentle, "Ah yes, missing the essence of the storm; an unfortunate event of many, but not you.

Let me start with the accounts of The Gahe," he continues. "These are the star beings of the Apache. I think you'll like this one," he says, as he gives me an entertaining squint. "They contain a history of a tribe which branched off from the majority of your people, and to this day take up residence within some of the deepest caverns here on earth, some which remain unexplored by man. The Gahe are supernatural beings who occupy caverns deep inside mountains in the lands of the Apache. It is said that they can sometimes be heard dancing and beating drums. They possess many powers, and are known to heal and drive away disease. In ritual dances of the Apache, masked dancers painted a different color for each point of the compass represent all the Gahe except the Grey One." With this, a smile widens on his face and he goes on, "the Grey One, a distant ancestor of yours, is the mightiest of all the Gahe, very respected and very revered amongst the Apache."

He continues in full stride, I assume with the intention not to let the growth of any possible pride I may have in this story create any kind of barrier that could shield me from, well, the essence of the storm. "The Pawnee Indians of the Great Plains of Nebraska were also known as The Star People. The heavens were a great influence on almost every aspect of their lives, and even their dwellings were constructed in patterns, which duplicated the patterns of the constellations, emphasizing the positions of their most important star gods. With the knowledge they received from these Sky Gods, using very humble astronomical observational tools in today's standards, they were able to observe and determine the motions of the moon, stars and planets; for they were very skillful sky watchers.

Proof of their great observational ingenuity still resides in the Pawnee collection at the Chicago Field Museum of Natural History. Ancient Pawnee sky charts were discovered wrapped in ceremonial objects that The Pawnee referred to as sacred bundles. The sacred bundles of the Pawnee were of such vital significance to the people that they were guarded and protected by the tribal shaman for their magical charms.

The bundle could be used to invoke the aid of The Great Spirit in times of famine, bringing buffalo to the tribe. It was told that these charts, made of an oval shaped piece of tanned elk skin, could be found in every Pawnee household within the sacred bundle; gifts from the stars. The beings who descended to Earth from the Heavens and delivered sky charts to the Pawnee descended to their people often, to maintain relationships with them and guide them." He inhales very deeply, surveys the coffee shop and then me, and inquires, "Would you like to resume at a later hour, tomorrow perhaps?"

"Alo listen," I begin, "The only thing I have scheduled on my extensive itinerary," I say, as I look at an invisible watch on my wrist, "is my regularly scheduled meeting with my pillow this evening. Now Mr. Pillow, understanding of my intense, daily obligatory pursuits, is extremely flexible and understanding. In fact," "To the Hopi, my people" he resumes, quickly internalizing my humor and even faster, dismissing it without even a hint of amusement, possibly taking offense to my sarcasm, "every aspect of life and death is governed by a different Kachina. The Kachina is responsible for the welfare of my people. These beings can assume the form of any physical object, phenomenon, or living being and come to us from a combined underground and sky realm separate from our home on the surface of the Earth."

Once again, he moves for his pipe. This time with no hesitation at all he begins to puff, and with a tremendous elimination of smoke he continues. "The Cherokee speak of Geyaguga, an all-powerful, magical spirit that descends from the moon. Achiyalatopa, the giant celestial monster with feathers of flint knives is known to the Zuni of western New Mexico. The Iroquois tell us that Ataentsic is the goddess of the earth, who fell from the sky. She is the creator of the sun and moon, and it is she who gives counsel in dreams." Taking another brief pause to puff, he seems to be in a summarizing mode at this point. After a few puffs, he extends his pause even longer, and sits back comfortably. Perhaps he is ready for my input. "Okay," he starts, "I believe you understand how important this subject is to my people. However, it is not only my people whose culture, and spirituality, incorporates accounts of interactions with sky gods that descend to us from the heavens. This has been happening since the inception of the human species. It is precisely the reason we are here."

The expression on his face prepares me for something deep, something it appears, that he wants me to retain with crystal clear clarity. "Hermeticism," he says. "Hermeticism is a religious and philosophical concept which affirms that a single, true theology exists and is present in all religions. It represents the understanding that this interconnected philosophy of all religions was given by the gods to man in antiquity. The religious minded and philosophers of spirituality can speculate and draw many connections to themes of what this concept truly is. However Travis, I am here to assure you that it is very clear that the foundation of any connection of the faiths here on this planet all began with one true genesis. Amongst the faiths, it is well documented that civilizations from other worlds have visited this planet for thousands of years. They are mentioned in mythology and scriptures from every continent.

On every continent and in every ancient civilization you can find stories about Star People or Sky Gods. The Incans, Mayans, Aztecs, Olmecs, Native Americans, far east traditions, Hindus, Aboriginals, African tribes, The Egyptians, The Ancient Greeks, European religions and even modern day Americans have these stories." He looks more deeply into my eyes, stopping to let the delivery of this verbal missive find its arrival in the proper destination of my intellect. "Hermeticism," he repeats.

CHAPTER 7

"*L*ook Alo," I hear myself express as I'm deep in thought about all of this, "it's not that I don't believe you, but, you say there's all this information and knowledge about all of this out there, so where is it? Now I'm not saying I'm the most learned person in New York or anything. Everybody can learn something new, but I'm smart, and I like to stay up on things." He doesn't respond, possibly contemplating the best explanation. "Look," I go on "I've just never heard of any of this before." Now I pause and brace for a rebuttal. It doesn't come, so I ask, "So what have you come across to, know all of this?"

With a content expression, a half smile forms across his face. He shifts a little in his chair as if preparing to recite something I assume he has recited a few times before, and begins, "Religion is very much a matter of vocabulary, you see. In almost every early civilization, beings descended from the heavens and had a hand in the development of the human race, with a promise to one day return. Some call them angels, others, spirits, and still others, gods. Today the scientific term of these otherworldly life forms is extraterrestrials, and out of the sky where these beings came, our ancestors referred to as the heavens.

Humans considered the technology of these extraterrestrials to be supernatural, and the beings themselves to be gods. An analogy could be drawn for this phenomenon with the cargo cults that formed during and after World War II, when once-isolated tribes in the South Pacific mistook the advanced American and Japanese soldiers for gods. One very important question remains. Why shouldn't these ancient accounts be interpreted as literal?" This question appears to be posed lacking the need for a response because he continues without waiting for any contribution from me. "These literal descriptions have become more obscure through the passing of many ages. Understand, it was the reactions of our ancestors to the contact with these beings that provided the origins of most religions on Earth today. Let me begin with the story of the earliest civilization known to man, the Sumerians. They inhabited the Fertile Crescent from about 3000 to 400 BCE. Theirs was a polytheistic nation. They believed in hundreds of different gods, male and female. Much of what we know about this Babylonian civilization has come from cuneiform tablets found in various ruins." Possibly anticipating another question, he quickly informs, "cuneiform script is one of the earliest known systems of writing. It was identified by marks wedged into clay tablets.

In 1849 cuneiform tablets were found archiving the Babylonian creation myth. This is the same myth in which the Bible draws its creation story of the first humans, however, the Bible leaves out many details. These same tablets also go into great depth about the lives of the Gods, referred to as the Anunnaki. Anunnaki means 'from Heaven to Earth they came.' It was written that the Anunnaki God Marduk took blood from the God Kingu and mixed it with clay to form the first humans.

The Sumerian capital of Err was discovered in 1853. This was the home of Abraham from the Bible, and there too, tablets were found which illustrated the Anunnaki as humanoid but not physical, although it was said that they could morph into human form. Still another Sumerian text, the Enuma Elish, explains the story of the Anunnaki as an advanced civilization that lived among them, and shared with them the wisdom of the gods." He looks at me as if for any confirmation that he has achieved the upper hand in the persuasion game, but I maintain a cool poker face.

His authenticity does seem right on point so far, and he has already convinced me that he is who he says he is, that's not why I hesitate. The truth is, I'm still a little freaked out by all of this. I mean, my body is transforming as we speak and I have no clue as to what exactly my future holds at this point. I'm not sure where I go from here, and I just want to dig a little further. I don't want to leave this table without a clear conscience and a plan, some sort of plan. If he is a guide, as he says, where is he going with all of this and what will my role be? I'm sure he's intent on covering the bases and pointing me in exactly the direction I need to go from here, I hope, but one thing seems to be more clear the longer we're here; my need for convincing seems to be diminishing the further he delves.

Heeding my reluctance, he presses, "Hinduism, the most ancient religion of our planet, gives great description of extraterrestrials, as well as space, interplanetary and time travel, parallel universes and the existence of life on other planets. Hindu texts provide the very blueprint of even the alien craft that they encountered, giving insight to the shapes and dimensions of the vehicles in which they witnessed in the sky. They speak of great wars between these extraterrestrial sky ships, and even detail the beams of light produced by these ships in war. They refer to these craft as Vimanas.

As in the scripture of other religions, Hindu text also provides a detailed exposition of interbreeding that occurred between man and these beings, in the story of Queen Kunti." He pauses, and somehow interpreting the question being formed in my mind, provides me with, "The Vedas, The Mahabharata, The Rigveda, The Ramayana and The Bhagavata Purana; these texts provide the proof of what I speak of. Understand that for the Hindus, the truth of the existence of other life strengthens a common belief in god's potential. It suggests that this potential can create whatever it desires, whenever it desires and wherever it sees fit.

The comprehension of this truth has allowed between Dinesh and I, a comfort and common ground in the ideology and knowledge of these sky beings, and is precisely why I was sent to you on his behalf." With that, he delivers a deep stare as if to signify his conquering of any disbelief of the authenticity he bears as a result of procuring this testimony over decades of enlightenment. Once again I must admit, his legitimacy slaps me across the face as it exhibits the insult of my ever questioning his authority. There's simply no denying that at this point, he's reeled me in line and hook. Now I'm more interested as ever to see which direction he will steer his presentation. I plant my elbow firmly on the table, and brace a fist along my face to display my submission to continue listening, and he welcomes the cue.

"Out of the same lands that Hinduism spawned," he says with a growing flare, most likely in recognition of his gaining of my respect, "Buddhism, another of the world's great religions, took hold and flourished. In the great Buddhist texts, the Acchariyabbhutadhamma Sutta and the Tipitaka, The Buddha himself gives reference to extraterrestrial life through spiritual revelations. He speaks of the black, gloomy regions of darkness between the world systems of intergalactic space and of the beings that inhabit these realms. The Buddha also gives great mention to life existing on other planets. Now, the Abrahamic religions offer perhaps some of the most intriguing discernment of the awareness of extraterrestrial life, and the interaction, which has taken place between humanity and these beings in the past. Many accounts are contained in both Christian and Islamic texts alike.

In The Bible, The story of Ezekiel's Wheel is one of the most descriptive texts you'll find about an alien visitation. As in the description of the Vimanas in Hindu text, Ezekiel describes in great detail the close encounter he had with the flying objects he witnessed descending out of the heavens. There are still many other examples. Both 2 Samuel 22:11 and Psalms 18:10 talk about God riding upon a celestial being that flew with wings. When God visited Moses he came down in rumbling fire. Matthew 28:2-3 tells that 'There was a violent earthquake, for an angel of the Lord came down from heaven and, going to the tomb, rolled back the stone and sat on it. His appearance was like lightning, and his clothes were white as snow.' This sounds much like the attire of our astronauts today. Luke 21:27 says, 'the Lord will come in a cloud with power and great glory.' Another significant aspect of extraterrestrial travel is also highlighted in the story of the resurrection.

It appears that after the resurrection in which Jesus ascended to Heaven, the angels and Jesus suddenly have the ability to appear and disappear as if they were traveling from other dimensions. In the book of Enoch, a book eventually taken out of The Bible, it describes Enoch's visits to heaven in the form of travels, visions and dreams, and his revelations. Many see this as a classic abduction story. Enoch was gone for 300 years. These accounts of unidentified crafts and other worldly technology witnessed by the ancients were their most natural interpretations, using what words and language they could to portray as clearly as possible these events in which they had no prior knowledge of. They are simply first-hand accounts of space travelers and the vehicles in which they came to Earth.

Just as in the Sumerian legends of the Anunnaki, the Bible speaks of how heavenly beings came to Earth and influenced the course of man's existence. Hebrews 1:14 poses the question, 'Are not the angels all ministering spirits, servants sent out in the service of God for the assistance of those who are to inherit salvation?' We see other examples again in the book of Enoch. Though as I said, we can no longer call The Book of Enoch a text of the Bible, the story of The Watchers provides one of the most vivid portrayals of extraterrestrial influence on humanity.

It reveals to us that 200 angels were chosen by God to watch over humanity. Through their interactions and over time, they became close to and fell in love with humans. They wanted to form bodies and mate with and marry humans, so they rebelled against God to accomplish this. Part of their rebellion was sharing the forbidden knowledge of God with humans. These angels descended from Heaven onto Mt. Hermon in Lebanon, on the border of Syria, and from here passed on to humans the knowledge of astronomy, metallurgy, magic, root cutting to create potions, medicine, science and even warfare.

There is a very interesting theme that The Watchers shared with other beings that came from the sky to pass on knowledge to mankind; they were depicted to look like serpents. We have a serpent story from the Bible in the Garden of Eden in which the serpent shared forbidden knowledge with humanity as well, and the Mayan god Kukulkan is a feathered serpent who brought them enlightenment. As you can see, each story of these serpent beings tells of them coming to earth and sharing with us the knowledge of the gods, which considerably advanced and civilized our race.

Christian beliefs also highlight the same potential of god that many Hindu philosophies suggest; a potential capable of creating all of existence. Colossians 1:16 -17 tells us that 'For by him were all things created, that are in heaven and that are on earth, visible and invisible, whether they be thrones, or dominions, or principalities, or powers; all things were created by him, and for him; and he is before all things, and by him all things consist.'" With this he stops and pats the pockets of his jacket, perhaps looking for his misplaced pipe. He looks at me sharply, "hungry?" he asks, as he pulls out a little paper bag he's concealed neatly in a front pocket.

"Umm, you know Alo, not really," I assure him as I sit back and adjust my now numbing left leg. "You go ahead, but thanks." He opens the bag and reveals some sort of pastry or muffin, which normally I wouldn't pass up, but with the whirling of the storm full force upon my intellect, nothing seems appetizing enough to pluck me from the eye of this beast. He eats contently for a few minutes, and I have no energy to contribute to any further conversation, so I wait patiently trying to navigate the squall that has enveloped my senses. After a few more munches, he starts in again with a mouthful of his last bite, "another of the Abrahamic religions, Islam, has its own interpretations of these celestial beings. The Quran makes reference to jinn and angels, which ascend to and descend from the heavens, both having the ability to take on human form.

One of the most important prayers to the Muslims, and the opening verses in the Quran instruct those of the Islamic faith to pray to God giving all praises and thanks due to the Lord of all creation, precisely suggesting that again, God has the potential to create all beings in existence." He grabs for a napkin and following a few swipes of his face, lets out a hearty belch, and then proceeds. "Surah Adh-Dhariyat, chapter 51 verse 47 informs us, 'and it is We who have built the universe with our creative power; and, verily, it is We who are steadily expanding it.'" After every verse he delivers, I notice he braces contently, and casts a stare into my eyes delineating that he has once again, delivered a swift connecting jab to the chin of my doubt.

"The Quran tells us," he goes on, "about multitudes of other planets where God's commandments are given there as well. The word seven in the Quran is used to denote a very large number, more like infinite, and Surah At-Talaq chapter 65 verse 12 explains of seven heavens and earths being created by God, and that Allah's 'command descends among them so you may know that Allah is over all things competent and that Allah has encompassed all things in knowledge.' This clearly highlights God's dominion over several different realms as well as creations, including our own.

Do you guys charge for water?" he asks abruptly, snapping me out of my thoughts, adrift in the flurry of the sea of my contemplation. "No, no, the cups are over there," I say as I point over my shoulder without turning to look. Feeling at the moment like he is my guest, even though he came to me,

I feel the need to ask, "Do you want me to grab you some?" "No need," he says as he reaches to place his hand on my shoulder, "an old man needs to stretch his legs. If I sit in this position any longer I'll be sure to get stuck that way. Then you'll have to pry me loose in front of everybody, and that's no easy task" he says with a smile. "I'll be right back."

"Joseph Smith Jr.," I hear from behind me as he approaches a few minutes later. "Huh?" I respond as he assumes his previous position directly across from me. He slides a cup of water my way, "Joseph, Smith, Jr.," he replies once more. "He is the founder of The Church of Jesus Christ of Latter-day Saints, also known as the Mormon Church. His experience shares virtually all the classic indicators of alien abduction. It shares many similarities with the abduction stories of people today.

It started with unusual dreams. Then one day, as he prayed in the woods near his home, he was engulfed in a beam of light and lost any ability to move. Many would dismiss this story and disregard the notion that God revealed himself to Joseph, particularly in a human form. So what was it that appeared to him that day? At the age of 17, a being appeared at his bedside claiming to be the angel Moroni. Moroni told Joseph that he had been sent to translate a book from plates of gold which Joseph was to find hidden in a hill near his home on an ancient Native American mound. Legend has it that many of these mounds can be found in North and South America, containing other similar plates, and where other plates have been found.

The significance of this story in mine is that, according to the book of Mormon, Moroni identified himself to Joseph Smith as a man who lived in America in the late 4th and early 5th centuries. However, Moroni himself claimed to be from the Pleiades star cluster. It is believed by some that Moroni revealed these findings to Smith because he wanted to pass on to Smith and his followers the advanced knowledge of mound building by Moroni's race. Mound building serves a very important purpose in communicating to future generations. It is as well, a tool used to communicate to those who visit other planets. The main message they present is the relaying of the precise origin of those who now inhabit a new planet, by mimicking the placement of the stars in which they came through their placement on the ground.

Throughout the world you can find several signs and monuments built to show us and anyone seeing them from above where many of the ancient relatives of the inhabitants of our civilization came from. For instance, within the geography of The Great Egyptian pyramids, the Mounds of Stonehenge, the design of many Mayan pyramids, the 7 Hills of Rome, the Lost Temples of Babylon, even 'the face' found on Mars, exists a precise and accurate architecture that mimics the precise alignment and brightness of the 7 stars of Pleiades, with the brightest star representing where some of our ancient relatives originated. Many other monuments have the same alignments with the constellation Orion, and several ancient stories tell of the vast numbers in which some of our ancestors' civilization came to Earth from these stars, as well as other parts of the universe. As you can see, another of the Earth's great religions began with extraterrestrial contact." With that, he undertakes a long pause, staring past me in deep reflection. An enormous sigh disperses from his lips, and he says, "This brings me to the conclusion of my story. It is the summary of three creations; the creation of your race as well as mine, and most important, the creation of religion."

CHAPTER 8

"*I* say story," he starts, "but realize, a story in my culture is a very factual account of our past. Just keep that in mind. Also, you must not lose sight of the fact that, though we, I say we as in man, were created by divine beings, creation has spawned from many makers and has produced many intelligent beings throughout the cosmos. There was life on Earth before the existence of modern man, and there are multitudes of life forms throughout the multiverse. Yes, there are many universes, and dimensions. If you believe only what science has taught you, science has already confirmed these truths. Another important aspect to never lose sight of is that, even though this is a story of our creation and the creation of our religions, our makers have their stories as well; their religions. For, they were made of beings more divine than themselves. Never lose sight of this knowledge."

He shifts in his chair and examines the coffee shop. As his eyes make their rounds of the room, their destination is brought about by a fixed gaze into my own. He appears as though he has a question to ask, or perhaps, he's finally awaiting my input. Maybe he's opening the floor for questions of my own. I don't know about in his culture, but in ours, this kind of a stare forces the opposition into a defense, so I give, "okay," I say, with the only thing I can muster at the moment, "so, why are we here?" He doesn't offer an immediate reply, and does not break his stare, so I clarify; "I mean, not you and I of course, I, I meant, why are people here, and where is everybody else out there?" This time, I decide to call his bluff, and I remain silent until he plays his hand.

Finally, he sits back comfortably, and begins. "I suspect there are a multitude of Alien civilizations visiting this Earth today. There are several varieties of space vehicles being reported, and the numbers of these reports are becoming more frequent every day. In addition, I myself have certainly encountered dozens of these beings. Most of them are friendly; if they wanted to take over this world they would have done so before humans invented weapons or any technology that they felt threatened by. The fact is, many have been sent to assist us in the development of life here on Earth, biologically and intellectually.

The Anunnaki were one of the first to arrive, and just as with your species, they had a significant role in human creation as well. It was only a matter of time before other advanced beings came upon the knowledge of what was happening on this little blue planet that they too decided to take part in the development of this world. Our species spawned from several of these other worldly, divine beings. This is why in many religions there is a reference to us being created in God's image. Along with the adaptation process of evolving in differing environments, one of the main reason we have so many varying races and ethnicities amongst our common DNA is because of the vast array of extraterrestrial civilizations that were able to cross their genetics with a common ancestor of ours. From what I have gathered over many decades of encounters, they each had, and still have different agendas for their involvement with our planet.

For instance, The Sumerian Tablets tell us that the Anunnaki needed to mine gold to form patches in their failing atmosphere. They landed on Earth in search of gold and found that gold was a very plentiful recourse of our planet. They also found much more here. They found life. Now understand, the Anunnaki possessed highly advanced knowledge of genetics and developed the concept of creating a worker being to help mine mass quantities of gold in order to save their planet. This is how the first recorded humans came to be. Even today, extraterrestrials are still experimenting with the human DNA and genes. In thousands of abduction reports, abductees' report of being the patients of these beings, and in sometimes-painful procedures, having eggs and sperm samples collected. To accomplish the development of the homo sapien, The Anunnaki took genes from a female hominid and after many, many trials, blended its DNA and theirs to make the first human beings. There is much scientific data to support this reality."

As he goes on, though I am fixated on every word that escapes his lips, I'm overwhelmed with the magnitude of all of this. As I begin to zone out, I hear his voice but the words are jumbled, and I get lost in deep comprehension of what exactly it is that is happening. There is so much to process, and it is all happening so quickly. If any of this is true, well at least some of it is true; obviously something is definitely happening to my body, what's going to happen to me? "Travis," I hear him call. "Travis," again he says. "Yeah, yeah I heard you," I begin, "but you didn't answer my question," he quickly chimes back. Not seeming too put off by my zoning, he says, "you're tired, I understand." "No it's not that," I assure him, "it's just, so much. I have a lot on my mind at the moment, you know?" "I understand Travis," he says with sincerity. "It is a lot, and that's why I'm here, as your guide, to help you make sense of all of it." "Well, what did you ask me again," I inquire.

"Darwin," he says, "have you ever heard of him?" "Isn't he the guy that talks about evolution," I throw out. "Very good," he replies with an approving nod. "Interestingly, in evolution there is a gap between pre-humans and modern humans. Many in the scientific field refer to this as Darwin's missing piece. We don't look anything like pre-humans, and our DNA seems to have literally changed overnight in the larger scheme of time. We came right out of the Stone Age and into science, medicine, math, kingship; every aspect of modern culture that we have today. This points directly to divine intervention, and for many, this is direct evidence of extraterrestrial influence on the creation of humanity.

In a scientific sense, the human genome is almost identical to a primate genome, with one very major exception. The second and third chromosomes are fused into one. So what does that solve? It gives you all of the chromosomal material of the primate but it's now only taking up the space of 46 chromosomes, while giving you 48 chromosomes of genomic material due to the fusion of the second and third chromosomes. The Anunnaki provided the other two chromosomes of genomic material, and thus, you have modern humans. In nature itself in any length of time, there would be no possibility of these chromosomes fusing. It was the direct engineering of the Anunnaki that accomplished this. This genetic engineering had one very significant implication. Eventually, it allowed these extraterrestrials to mate directly with humans.

You can find confirmation of this in many religious texts and within several of the legends of early civilizations. Ancient Greek mythology spoke of many Gods mating with humans, producing what they called demi gods such as Hercules and Perseus. Genesis chapter 6 and Numbers chapter 13 speak of The Nephilites. The Nephilim were the offspring of angels known as the sons of God, and the daughters of men, human women. They were giants, and inhabited the lands of Canaan. They were said to be heroic warriors and men of renown.

Many consider the story of Mary of Nazareth from the Bible, the mother of Jesus, to be key proof of the involvement of extraterrestrials with the cross engineering of their DNA and that of human DNA. This story very much implies the direct breeding of celestial beings with humans. Traditionally, Christians hold the belief that Mary conceived Jesus through what they referred to as 'divine intervention' of the Holy Spirit. Muslims believe that this miraculous conception was the result of the command of God.

Interestingly, this occurred when Mary was already betrothed to Saint Joseph and was awaiting the final marriage rite of the formal home-taking ceremony. After this, she accompanied Joseph to Bethlehem where Jesus was born. Also, let us also not forget the story of The Watchers from the book of Enoch, who fell from Heaven and mated with humans.

Even in our native tradition," he goes on as he focuses his eyes in storyteller fashion, at the same time producing the onset of a proud smile, "we have knowledge dating back to antiquity which explains that the gods descended from heaven to impregnate barren females in remote villages. The mothers bearing these special seeds would then nurture and raise these, 'Star Children,' until about the age of six. At this time, the gods were said to return to reclaim their offspring, leaving villagers staring up into the infinite beyond.

Now getting back to the Anunnaki, in 1927 the Sumerian Queen Puabi was found in southeast Iraq. The significance of this finding is that her skull was abnormally large, resembling skulls from mummies found in Peru as well as some of the skulls of Egyptian Pharos. These findings point to a direct connection that these were some of the first descendants of the hominid and Anunnaki offspring. Even the Mayan civilization, thousands of years later, reported being visited by the Anunnaki, and they too were known for having the same shaped skulls. This is no coincidence you see.

Another very relevant finding shows further proof of the influence of Anunnaki genes on humanity. The Sumerian King list, which the Bible pulls from, speaks of 140 kings who lived for hundreds and thousands of years. The reason for the long lifespans of these early people is because these original humans were closer in genetics to the Anunnaki, who lived even longer. As genes adapt and change to meet the conditions of the environment, and in response to quality of life, our lifespans shortened.

Now, Sumerian legend tells us that after our creation, the Anunnaki saw how fast and with what great ability humans learned and developed, and saw this ultimately as legitimizing the positivity of their influence on our creation, and they were very pleased. However, over time they began to also notice that as the humans developed, the power we possessed increased. With this increase in power, the Anunnaki noticed an increase in man's negative aspects as well. With power, man tended to become more evil and corrupt.

The Anunnaki leader, Enlil, saw this as an opportunity to get rid of Mankind and its evil doings. This is very similar to the Tower of Babel story in the Bible, and also to how ancient man rose up to rival the god's and titans in Greek tradition. Now Enlil's brother, Enki, saw the possibilities of mankind being able to overcome this nature, and plotted to rescue mankind by instructing his faithful devotee, Utnapishtim, who is Noah from the Bible, to build a submersible ship that would save himself and his family. This is the reason why we have a flood story in almost every religion and civilization. Coming to terms with our survival, the Anunnaki developed a new plan of cultivating us further so that we could possibly live in harmony with them and the rest of creation. They vowed to one-day return to us in the future. This is another common theme in many religions; the return of God.

The Anunnaki have been visiting, leaving and returning to Earth now for millions of years. Their home planet, Nibiru, has an orbit so large that it comes into the Milky Way and close enough to us for them to land on Earth about every 3,450 years. Scientists estimate that the next time it will make a pass by our planet will be in 2900. Interestingly, with every visit by the Anunnaki, we receive great enlightenment and become vastly more technological. They spoke of Nibiru as a star, a gate and a crossing place; a place containing wormholes and stargates by which they traveled the cosmos. As I've mentioned, they've promised to return. Now, if the Anunnaki are the gods spoken about in all these ancient texts, then it is probable that they would have also created many other races as well."

He shifts again in his chair, seeming to prepare to switch gears, and I take this opportunity to stretch and readjust. "With this promise to one day return to us in mind then," he goes on, "it makes sense that they would have quite an interest in us. We certainly may well be one of their grandest experiments." He leans in a little, and stares into my eyes. "The Greys," he says with a stern gaze, "were created by the Anunnaki to oversee the development of humanity. They were permitted to conduct experiments and tests and to gather and record vital information to relay back to the Anunnaki about mankind. The Greys are your people.

From my contacts with The Greys, it appears they are not hostile, although just as with anything in the universe, they too are capable of the traits of good and evil. To carry out their job as watchers over humanity, they have set up lunar bases on the dark side of the moon. Of course from Earth we cannot see or track that side of the moon because the moon does not rotate on an axis like our Earth. That side is naturally shielded from our sight. The governments of the world have knowledge of your people, and have used the technology they've recovered from them to make military advancements and to refine our own technology.

Astronauts of the Apollo missions have confirmed knowledge of these bases and contact with the beings that inhabited them, which has remained concealed information from the public for decades. Even today, interaction with and testing of our species by yours is a very current affair.

As I alluded to earlier, many abductees have reported about The Greys and the painful procedures they undergo to have reproductive tissues, eggs, sperm and other cells removed and sampled. Furthermore, many have reported being subjects of metallic chips being implanted in parts of their bodies, which they believe to be some sort of tracking devices; similar to the devices we place on the animal populations we are tracking. Several doctors and scientists around the world who have encountered these abductees have not been able to identify this chip of being made with any earthly material, and every time were unsuccessful in their attempts to remove these chips.

One thing that may comfort you, Travis, is coming to the realization that you are not the only, alien, to dwell among us today. Many religions have had this knowledge for centuries. The Bible says, 'do not neglect to show hospitality to strangers, for by this some have entertained angels without knowing it;' angels in other words being extraterrestrials." It appears the time has come for an intermission. As he's done several times tonight, he reaches for his pipe and begins to take little puffs. I've noticed that he does this prior to revealing some of his most crucial information. The thoughts of his peyote speech have all of the sudden resurfaced to the top of my awareness.

"Traditionally peyote is used in pursuit of religious ceremonies. Understand, rituals can be conducted by oneself and with the creator, with a guide, a group, at any place, or time the creator and the participant deem necessary." For Alo, this is his calling, and it is a very spiritual pursuit indeed. They peyote appears to connect him with the highest heights of his consciousness, bestowing upon him the ability to guide those he's been sent to with the most precise clarity and authority, allowing them to receive his message, and to perceive every step of their appointed path with full intent.

After a few seconds of sporting a meditative look upon his face, he opens his eyes with a relaxed aura, and continues, "These extraterrestrials, with their advanced civilizations and possessing other worldly technology, would truly be God's to ancient man. Their civilizations span millions of years even prior to human existence, and to them, the every detail of this macrocosm we know of as space is of no mystery. They have witnessed many worlds come and go. They have knowledge so advanced that not even the most imaginative creations of human science fiction can begin to portray the capacities of their technology. The Anunnaki are very aware of the evolutionary steps cognition has to go through. Knowing how young of a species humanity really is, this is a very crucial topic for them. As children growing up under the microscope of their parents, they want to protect us. After all, when you have become God, you don't want to see your creation destroyed. In addition, they know the importance of nourishing our growth and development so that we can truly have a place in the universe, and coexist in peace and harmony with the rest of creation. This, as you can see, is the crux of religion.

Religion was passed to us simply as a tool for them to track human cognition. What better barometer could be used to measure the development of learning, understanding, perception, discernment and insight? With religion, you have intellectual concepts, abstract ideas, emotions and morality and the deepest discernment of insight the imagination can produce. You have a platform from which to enhance every aspect of cognition, and to be able to measure and interpret what this cognition is capable of and can produce for future generations.

Realize this however, just because we were created by them, doesn't discount the fact that we have spirits, and souls. The simplest component of our being is the collection of electrons, precisely energy, and science has proven that any energy that is created can never be destroyed; only transformed. This suggests that some component of our existence will always go on you see. This creating of beings by other beings is one of the great realities of the cosmos. This cycle of beings creating beings has been occurring for millennia. We are creations of them, and we are now advanced enough ourselves to manipulate genes as they did.

We too, now possess the ability to create life, to, play God some claim. However, something else that you must, you must be mindful of, is that, though the handing down of religion to us was a ploy, a strategy by them to help humanity grow into elite beings, it does not discount the fact that the root of spirituality stems from one true genesis. Even to those who passed it to us, the divinity of a most supreme force was unveiled to their most primordial predecessors near the beginning of time. This is the source of any modern religion, anywhere in the cosmos. Over many eons, religion has been slowly spread throughout the cosmos, taking on different forms and interpretations, in very sparse pockets here and there. Still, the vast majority of the multiverse is still without, religion.

The main reason they haven't revealed these truths to humanity yet is simply because, in the larger realm of time and space, we are still a very primitive civilization. In their view, we have no respect for life, the ideas of other races and cultures, which could mean a blatant disregard to accept the ideas of any other intelligent beings we would encounter. Furthermore, we have not become masters of our emotions. In this light, unable to govern ourselves with brotherhood, with killing and warfare loose on the Earth in the name of religion, they will not allow us to become part of the celestial neighborhood that is our cosmos. Nor will they openly reveal themselves to us. In time, this is their aim, but as long as we remain ignorant and naïve, fighting over whose religion is the right one, or the best, and choose exclusivity as our means to a solution, we will remain in the dark, alone and isolated from the rest of creation. They will not allow us to traverse the universe in search to conquer and convert other species in the name of religion, as we have done on our own planet. We are still a work in progress, and our willingness to accept a peaceful approach to inter-religious understanding will determine our future position in the cosmos.

From my own several decades of experience with the many different beings I've come across, similar themes arise and connect each form of spirituality they all possess. The ideas of certain practices that allow one to control the untamed and undisciplined conscience, a conscience that can give way to the germ of selfishness, trouble and evil, is a core concept of many faiths. The creeds of love, peace, discipline, ethics, wisdom, compassion and the attainment of true happiness seem all to be central to the development of any strong sense of spirituality amongst all of the civilizations' religions I've encountered. You see, each religion shares common foundational beliefs, but on Earth, it has been the doctrines and rituals and lists and numbers of each religion that have caused the main rift between the acceptance of what similarities join each faith at the core.

The appeal of His Holiness the Dali Lama to humanity can sum up the approach humanity must take to find a place and a permanent identity in concert with the rest of the creation in the multiverse. He pleads that 'the only appropriate, responsible, and effective way to live in this undeniable reality is to follow the principles of compassion.' Only then will the God's reveal themselves." With this last statement, he sits back, staring off into the distance without further regard of my presence, as if he is reassuring himself of this belief. This seems to signify his closing because he waits, and waits, possibly for any sign of an unwavering conviction to his testimony on my behalf.

There is something however that is resonating in my mind at the moment. To break the silence and to quench the thirst of my confusion, I break in with, "okay, but, there's one thing Alo. If my race is so much more, advanced than yours, and we've been appointed as your, keepers, for the time being at least, then why have we been allowed to live in harmony with these other beings without religion, since this is such an important criterion for the acceptance into the extraterrestrial community?" With an immediate change in his expression, as if I was an alarm clock that has chimed in to attribute to something he had forgotten to address, he says, "Your race has been allowed a place simply based on its compassion, even in the absence of their own faith.

Religion was also bestowed upon them, but your race, as one of the most technologically advanced, has become so scientific and advanced that they lost their imagination. They lost their religion, and ultimately, their happiness.

They failed to see that even science started with a thought, a concept; it started with imagination, and that's what they lost. It is this, imagination, which is a central component of any religion. We call it faith. Now, in a turn of events, they're looking to the stars. They're looking to us, for enlightenment. The birth of every faith begins with a messiah, a prophet, and now, the key to a new age of spirituality lies with you Travis. You can be a savior to many."

CHAPTER 9

*I*t's been exactly a month since my conversation with Alo that evening in the coffee shop, exactly the same amount of time that Alo said would elapse before he would return to take me to where I needed to go; a point in which, from Earth, would allow me to teleport back to my home planet. Our conversation ended about as abruptly as it had begun the day we met. He seemed to be in a hurry to get somewhere after the last bit of words he exchanged with me, and informed me that he would find me in exactly one month to take me where I would need to go to send me home. I've hardly slept a solid wink since then, and have been pretty much navigating my existence in a sort of zombie mode, wrapped up in this whirlwind my life has been swept into within the last few months.

One thing that has had a definite impact on me since then however, is this role I am supposed to carry out in all of this. After going through this intense religious boot camp, I've come to realize that, although I understand there is a very important requirement for religion within any civilization, it has also become clear that if it's not focused correctly and carried out in a way that allows others to freely express their spirituality, within a society of compassion and tolerance, religion can cause the opposite of many of the outcomes it pursues to promote. If everything works out as it is supposed to, and I make it back, I believe this will be the grandest ideal I will pass down to my people.

Today has been a pretty normal day, except for me obscuring this pact that Alo has formed with me from the rest of the world, a pact that is supposed to come to fruition any moment. I don't recall him giving me a time frame. I just got off of work, and I scan the coffee shop for any sign of him. I see some regulars, some people I haven't seen before, but no Alo. I head out of the back door as usual and make for my apartment. As I approach my building I see a figure standing by the entrance staring in my direction. The closer I get, I make him out. "How did you know where I lived?" I inquire as I reach him. "Hello Travis," he responds. "Have you forgotten all about me?" he asks with a grin bent with sarcasm. "I'm your guide, remember?" He follows. Not surprised by this response I say, "yeah, okay," as I open the door in pursuit of the stairwell I frequent on my every return home.

Halfway up the stairs I hear, "that, is the wrong way Travis." "What?" I yell as I turn toward him, "I just got off of work Alo. You mean we have to go now?" "No," he looks up at me, with a somewhat regretful, sorrowful expression, and then goes on, "no, there is no longer a need for that. My only aim is to speak with you." "Huh, wait?" I immediately blurt, a little aggravated between the exhaustion overcoming me from my lack of sleep in combination with his vagueness. "What do you mean speak to me? Was this all a fucking joke?" I hear myself scream. "We can talk right here, we don't need to go anywhere!"

After a brief interlude, with a scowl he begins, "Your people, your planet, is no more." I return a scowl his way as my eyes begin to widen. This must have all been a joke. He begins to approach me and he says, "Lack of religion caused many of your kind to abandon regard for their happiness, abandon regard for the need of any sort of salvation or liberation, and abandon compassion, morality and the desire for survival itself." The closer he gets climbing the stairs towards me, his eyes seem ablaze. "Ultimately," he continues, "this lack of faith, this abandonment of spirituality has resulted in yet another world destroyed. Some of your people have managed to escape to remote outposts on other planets with a similar atmosphere and landmass as your own. These few still hold the belief in your race to recover its lost spirituality, and its desire to continue to thrive and repopulate the cosmos. He's within an arm's reach of me now.

He reaches toward me and places his palm on the area right above my heart. As I look down at his hand my vision immediately becomes blurry and I begin to lose all sensation. I find myself in a pitch-black realm, as floating without my body, and in the distance I make out a scene. As it begins to grow and become clearer, it is a scene of my planet. In an immense rapidity, the whole history of my planet from its inception to its golden eras, through its loss of religion and its ultimate destruction, in what seemed to be a few seconds, has been revealed in this supernatural account and has been transferred and imprinted into my mind as if I've watched this movie hundreds of times, and now have every detail of it engrained in my cognition ready for recall. As I come to, I realize I'm staring at the ceiling, and as I sit up and drowsily glance down the stairwell, I see the shadowy figure of Alo's back standing in the dim light of the doorway at the bottom of the stairs. "Travis," he begins, "I can help. You now understand the implications of what colossal power and influence religion has on all of creation, and you, you have the power within obtaining this knowledge to save many others. You have the faculty, along with my assistance if you so desire, to spread this message to others, to spread, the faith of the cosmos." He disappears into the bustling Brooklyn evening.

INTRODUCTION TO STORY 2

*I*n the months that followed Travis' account, the universe went to work

elsewhere, in a very different way. Forces were in motion, in preparation for

something much larger, much more, impactful and important. Unbeknownst

to many, the course of humanity was already vastly entrenched in a process of

immense transformation. This transformation, when it is brought to fruition,

will prove to be of most monumental proportions, and will be reflected in

every form of the human condition. At this point in time, the story of

humanity's role in it all is in its infancy. The next account, the story of Seth,

helps to set the framework for this vast awakening that is about to take place

throughout the Universe, and what it means for humanity's place in the

cosmos. This is The Elucidation of Star Beings Part 2: Seth

THE ELUCIDATION OF STAR BEINGS
PART 2: SETH

CHAPTER 1

*A*s the cool breeze tickles the skin of my face, I can't help but think to myself, 'how in the world did I get this life?' I'm riding with my top down in a Rolls-Royce Phantom Drophead Coupe, slate clay and cadet blue interior with a Gainsboro paint job, not to mention, fresh off the lot. I'm on my home to show it off to my family where my wife and daughter are patiently awaiting my return. They knew I was planning on coming back home with something special. It was just one of those days you know? Well maybe you don't, but I get those days where I just want to go and spend some money; treat myself. I work hard and play harder. Plus, when you're pulling in over 700k a year as a combined income, what else are you supposed to do with it all?

As I get closer to our home, well, our mansion, nicely nestled in the west hills, I smell the sweet aroma of freshly cut grass and feel the gentle caress of the very comfortable July sun hugging me tightly. At the moment I'm lost in a daze of autopilot, examining in my mind the next big purchase, and how lucky, well, fortunate; I don't believe in luck. Anyway, I'm thinking of how fortunate I am to have so much, and you know what, I deserve it. There's a reason I'm up here in the hills, above the poverty and crime that erodes downtown Portland. I don't belong down there with them. I stay away from Burnside, Alberta, MLK, most of the east side and some parts of the park blocks downtown, unless of course I have to venture into some of those god forbidden areas on an errand or two. Then again, I guess it could be a lot worst. Portland is a great place to raise kids. The crime rate is fairly low compared to most cities, and there are plenty of good schools. It's a little slow for me here though, and unbeknownst to my wife, when the kids get old enough, I'm buying a house somewhere tropical where I'll spend most of my time. I did say kids. She's about to pop any day now with my first son. I love my daughter, but I've been waiting on this little guy for some time now. I don't play the favorites game of course, but I was sweating bullets waiting to have an heir to my throne, you know, someone to pass on the coveted name of the Walkers.

As I approach our drive and pull up to the gate, I notice my daughter dismiss the beach ball she was kicking around the yard and head towards me while screaming, "daddy, daddy," in full stride. My Doberman decided that the ball would be his next victim and has just made a kill, as I see the ball shriveling in his jaws while he shakes it to its last breath. 89865, I punch in the keypad. As I pull my new toy into its new home behind the other cars, I see my wife peeking out of the doorway. As I park and slip off my Maui Jim's, I catch a grin across her face that expresses exactly the thought that her mind has immediately formed; "figures," exclaims the smirk she now sports.

As we are locked in a stare down, I hear the piercing scream of my daughter on the passenger side of the car, "Gino ate my ball. He ate it daddy, it's mine!" she screams, as she runs around to my door. "Honey, daddy will buy you a new one today okay? What color do you want?" I ask in my most comforting voice, while trying to hold back the fact that I actually got a kick out my fierce guard dog protecting his home against the dangers of the colorful plastic lump that was the ball. "I want the same color daddy, the same exact one okay?" she says as she jumps into my arms. "I can do that for you hun, okay?" I assure her, "I got it covered, just for you, now go play baby."

I see my wife disappear behind my daughter through the front door, and I take the opportunity to reflect a bit in the dazzling evening glow. Let's see, I have a gorgeous wife; a short, very fit, petite little piece of beauty, with curves in all the right places, a healthy, beautiful, intelligent little girl with bouncing curlicues for hair, and hazel eyes, a boy to match on the way, this dream home that we just moved into; I even have the dog. My very existence is the epitome of the American Dream. However, there is one problem; something that I'm reminded of like an itch in the middle of my back that I can never scratch. I'm still not satisfied. The desire for more hasn't stifled in the slightest with the accumulation of my upper class status.

This beast grows in the ever-brewing cauldron of my acquisitive materialism. It's like somehow this burning rage to acquire more has been genetically engineered into my make-up. I've heard that I have an obsessive, addictive personality more than once. "It's a product of growing up so affluent and privileged," they say. "Money can't buy you happiness, keep that in mind," is the buzzing phrase amongst those who have less to show for. In my opinion, it's just all those lazy fuckers' way of justifying what they don't have. As I lay back across my seat, the smell of new car invades my nostrils and approves of my thoughts with the advance of its sweet aroma.

Dinner, somehow this is the next thought that manifests itself in my present muse. Rough life huh? These are the things that I have to internally struggle over, not whether I'll have enough money to cover rent every month, or how in the world I'll feed my kids for the next few days. I never have to be anxious or stressed about not being able to have a Thanksgiving or Christmas, or if I won't be able to afford the newest and up to date technological wonders that seem to introduce themselves to the world every 18 months or so. Well, I do get concerned sometimes with how many taxes the greedy governors of Oregon will extract from my income during tax season, but all in all, I've pretty much got it made and life is good, very good.

"Dinner time! Come on in Seth. Oh, and I have your meds, it's that time," I hear from across the lawn. That's Rosie, our maid. She's a feisty little Cuban lady, and about the only one around here who seems to be able to contain my ego. You have to understand, this woman waits on our family hand and foot, so I feel like I owe her some humility, but I'll tell you, she's about the only one I feel that way about. It's true; Rosie possesses a lot of power in a weird sort of way. I feel like my empire would crumble if it wasn't for her. She's a little more than just a maid. She's a babysitter, she acts as one of my accountants, our secretary, tutor, cook, nurse, plus, it doesn't hurt that she's bilingual. Elli, my daughter, has picked up a good amount of Spanish from her. I've already instilled in Elli how important this will be for her career, at the ripe old age of 4.

My meds; yes, the king of the castle does have a little anxiety issue. My blood pressure is slightly high and my doctor says my LDL is so high I'm a walking time bomb. My triglycerides are through the roof. It doesn't help that I have a little Jager habit, my bimonthly casino excursions throw me to the Eden of second hand smoke, and Rosie keeps my freezer stocked with Ben and Jerry's Heath Bar Crunch ice cream that I frequent nightly, usually at around 2 in the morning for some reason. Thus, Rosie is the keeper to the box of meds that thrusts me amongst the ranks of so many Americans these days. I guess you could say the sad part about all of this is I'm a doctor myself, and I should probably know better. That's actually the reason why we moved down to Portland from Seattle. I was offered a job as an Anesthesiologist at the Oregon Health & Science University, and there's no way on Earth I could pass up the offer; money talks, and I've been very blessed. Wait, blessed might not be the right word; it's so, qluiche.

Besides, I'm not really a religious person. I find I don't have too much patience for the concepts and theories of the religious minded. Who's right? Who's wrong? How many times are we supposed to pray? Are we supposed to attend church? Is it okay to do this? Is it okay to do that? What happens when we die? Who cares anyway? How does any of that help me now? I don't know, maybe one day I'll hire someone to explain all this to me, or just do my own research; maybe when I'm retired I'll slow down a little and focus on these farcical, fantasy philosophies of people that haven't reached their true potential and need a source of motivation to keep going. In the meantime, I'll stay focused on my assets and trust funds. That's my reason for waking up every day, well, besides my family of course, but I mean, money is absolutely my passion. It has bought me a life of luxury, and I'm the happiest man in the world because of my financial security. Who needs religion when they've reached the pinnacle of happiness, and without the help of some all-powerful deity floating above us somewhere in the stars.

"Your meds are on the counter by your paper," Rosie says as I enter the front door. "The fish oil," she continues, "is in the little Dixie cup as usual. The Paxil and Lasix are in the pill holder, and your," all of the sudden I tune her words out, well; I don't intentionally tune them out. Something does, and I begin to daydream, if that's what you want to call it. Everything in my peripheral transforms into a dark grey haze, and Rosie becomes the focal point of very blurry tunnel vision. Her words have diminished into a slow motion ramble that is almost inaudible. Then I pick up on her words again as I feel a growing, drowsy daze make its way up my body to my head. "Okay Dr., IV has been administered and the naloxone is ready." In the deeper voice of a male, she continues, "he may need gastric lavage, so make sure we're ready team." For a second I try to blink hard, as if that will magically clear up the blur as well as the claptrap that escapes from this little woman in front of me. "He may need some psychiatric evaluation once this is all over," she continues. Again, this time in the voice of the young woman, she goes on, "well remember, it's your first night here, so it's my job to make you as comfortable as possible. Don't worry, I'll be watching over you." With that I come out of the delusion. I don't respond, and I'm a little creeped out by the blank stare she exhibits as I turn to leave. In reality, it's me, I mean, my imagination, but I'm too scared to actually reveal this to Rosie so I turn and head up the stairs.

I love the summer, but it's nearing 8 PM and it's still as bright as any afternoon. Right now, I need it dark. I've got to be exhausted. The move, the stress, the anticipation, money; they're all weighing so heavy on my mind at the moment I can barely focus and I can feel the calm of my heart before a possible storm I'm trying ever so desperately to avert. I need to relax. As I stare out of the master bedroom window overlooking our backyard, I catch a glimpse of my pregnant wife attempting to push Elli on the swing and begin to feel light headed and short of breath. With that, I close the blinds. I feel my head lightly thump the goose down pillow on my side of the bed. I close my eyes. At this rate, I could be in for a long week. It's Sunday and I go back to work tomorrow.

CHAPTER 2

What a day, and not the least bit in a good way either. I must have slept for about 9 hours yesterday, but I feel like I haven't slept a wink. I'm exhausted and I feel a numb sort of weakness today. At times throughout the day my fatigue was so great I had trouble keeping my balance here and there. I'm starting to get a little concerned because I've felt tired before, plenty tired, but this feels like something else; almost unbearable.

Sometimes I wonder why I ever decided to be an anesthesiologist. The hours are unpredictable. I obviously have to be available for the elective surgeries on my schedule, but then again, it's the hospital, and the emergency room can call anytime; childbirth, heart attacks, car accidents, it's all part of the job. I guess that's what happens when the only objective of putting yourself through school for a career is motivated solely by compensation. Then again, I guess I could have decided on a career such as a Business Development Director like my wife, and work from home most of the time. Now that's something I could get used to. Anyhow, like I said, what a day.

I got to the hospital this morning around 6:15. The first thing I always do is check to see where I have been assigned for the day. I may be in an operating room or in our pre-op area interviewing patients and preparing them for surgery. Sometimes I get obstetrics, and things always have the potential for a good time in there, and by good I mean hectic. Today, I got stuck with the high stress task of being in charge of the operating room. Then, at about 2:30 I was notified that I was needed in the ER, where I remained until about, well, now. It's 7PM. I'm tired, starving and I just want to be home.

Normally on my way home I take the city route, as I did tonight. This takes me up Burnside a ways and connects me to my yellow brick road that is Barnes, which delivers me up the massive hill toward my neighborhood in the west hills like an elevator ascending out of the mouth of the impoverished pockets of Portland that rear their toothless smiles at me daily as I drive past. For some reason, today while stopped at a light I was drawn to a building as if a puppeteer turned my head with plucks of an imaginary string, so that this place would come directly into my line of sight. I must have driven by this building dozens of times, but today, I'm not sure why I had the intense urge to look at it. It's almost like it called to me, and as it did, took control of my motor skills with a relentless force.

As soon as my eyes rested upon its walls I get the feeling that I've seen this place before, been inside of it, but that's impossible. With an intense flash I see inside of it. Well, inside of somewhere. I'm not sure if it was the inside of this building, but somehow it evoked a most vivid sight of a room, with several young men in a food hall. As my eyes travel the room I see counselors reprimanding some, others, huddled with a few boys in a line waiting for a meal. Just then the toot of a car horn snaps me out of this illusion producing another jolting flash. I rub my eyes and shield them from the bright light of the western setting evening summer sun making its way behind the direction of my home. Where are my sunglasses? Anyway, I better go before I cause too much of a ruckus. As I lightly tap the gas pedal another flash thrusts my foot harder against the pedal and a vision of a sign that says Father Flanagan's Boys Home streaks across my plane of sight and disappears in an instant. I hit the brakes, with my bumper attempting to kiss the fender of the car in front of me. What a day.

As the gate swings open and reveals my driveway, I notice that there's an unusual display of lighting around the kitchen and dining room, and as I turn off the car I can hear laughter and loud voices conversing in over-exited tones. Was Tamara having a work event or something? Tamara is my wife by the way. She's usually good about informing me of these things beforehand, but maybe with the move and all of the new developments we have in the works, there's a possibility that she overlooked having that conversation with me. With this thought in mind, I realize that I'm not ready to entertain any guests at the moment; I'm dragging. Maybe I should just take a nap right here, right now. As I slip my head back and shift my body into a comfortable position, I lower the seat to a nice incline. This is more like it. Shit, it's John!

I forgot that I invited one of my best friends from high school who had just recently moved to Portland from Minnesota where he had took up residence for the last 10 years. He met his wife there, and they had two little boys. He and I came across each other's profiles recently on Facebook after not talking for many years, and he said that they too had just moved to Portland. The plan was that they were going to "welcome" us and come have dinner tonight; let the families mingle a bit. I told him 5 o'clock sharp. I turn on the car to check the time; 8. With an untapped reserve of adrenaline I had hidden somewhere in the depths of my body, I muster a burst of vigor that launches me up and out of the car. As I trot toward the door, I imagine the scene of Tamara and I arguing later about my lack of punctuality, and an intense play of how I'll have to defend myself by replaying my day presents itself into my field of vision. All of the sudden I feel a sharp throb form a crown around my head. My heart is pounding and I need a second, so I brace myself on the porch before I enter.

Just then the door swings open and Tamara shoots a glare at me, which affirms the revelation I've just had. She doesn't say a word, but then I notice the anger on her face turn into a confused concern as she sees me slumped over. "Seth?" she starts in. "I'm fine honey," I assure her. "Well hurry up and come in then," she responds with a widening of her eyes and a summons in with a hurried wave.

After the, festivities, if you want to call them that; you know, introducing the families, boasting about our achievements, which I have to say ours heavily outweighed theirs, talking about old times and of course, feasting, I ask John if he wants to come and check out my man cave. I have a small theater room where I've put a few other goodies like a pool table, a bar and a poker table. Sitting on the bar seats with a little background noise from ESPN, John looks over at me and says, "well Seth, I'm impressed, very. It's crazy really when you think of where we've come from and where we are now." He's done pretty well for himself. He spent his first 8 years in Minnesota as a longshoreman, making a pretty little chunk of change. In his last 2 years he landed a job as a First-Line Supervisor of Fire Fighting and Prevention Workers, "pulling in a little over 90,000 a year," in his words. I'm assuming it's a little less than that, as men naturally tend to add a generous sum to the real number of what their income represents. Anyway, he transferred out to Portland to be closer to his family, and enjoys it here.

"I mean look at you!" he goes on. "This is wonderful Seth," and as he lowers both his gaze and his voice, with a nudge of an elbow into my side he throws in, "must be nice huh, to be one of the privileged few? I wouldn't know about that," he laughs. "Hey, I'm not blaming you though, if you got it, use it." Something about that comment immediately sends a tingling warmth throughout my face, and contorts my features. I'm sure had I been staring back at myself I would have been revealing the snarling canines of Kujo. "What the fuck is that supposed to mean, huh?" I scream as I rise to my feet effortlessly. "You know what? That's the fucking problem with America these days. It's become the land of lazy bastards who want to live off of the government, and guess who gets to pay for that. Don't blame me for coming from a storied family of go-getters; people who have worked a lifetime to better the future of their family name, honest, hardworking people. Privileged is what those who are full of excuses and failures like to call it! John, you're one of them, to a T. You come from a long line of losers. You're a loser, and your kids will follow suit," I snarl as the foam that's built up in the corner of my mouth propels itself in all directions.

As soon as the words have left my lips I realize that they came out so fast I hadn't really had a chance to process the gravity they carried. It was almost as if there was a microscopic recorder in my mouth with a giant finger planted firmly on the play button. I didn't even have to think of the words. They were just a part of the playback. What have I done? However, for some reason I'm still very, very angry, and confused. "Seth," he says as his joking demeanor has now given way to discuss, "that's not what I meant, at all, but I thank you for your honest opinion." He gets up and takes a few steps toward the door, and without turning says, "welcome to Portland," and then walks out of the room. In his absence I can feel tears welling up and in response, a sour soreness forms in my throat as I try to hold them back. "Is everything okay Seth?" I hear a voice. "John and Kathy are leaving," says Tamara in nothing more than a whisper.

"I'm going to the study," is about the only thing I can think to say. "Seth, you've not been yourself lately. Aren't you going to at least say bye, or would you like me to take care of that as well?" she says. "Now is not the time Tamara." I can feel the warmth of wrath begin to possess my body once more. "You know what, I'm tired of your smart ass, rude comments, and I'm really tired of those little faces you like to make. Can't you see how hard I've been working, huh? I'm tired," I hear myself scream. "I know it's hard for you to be a supportive wife at this point, and you like to blame everything on the fucking pregnancy like that gives you a reason to act like a bitch, but I'm done with that shit. I'll be in the study and I suggest you not follow. I pass her without looking at her, for some reason afraid to read across her face the damage of what my words have inflicted.

As I sit alone in my thoughts, trying to sift through what had actually transpired this evening, I hear the study door creek open a little, and turn to see Elli with her favorite cozy. That's what we call it. It's a little blanket her grandmother made for her. "Daddy," she squeaks. "Yes dear," I hear myself respond, still somewhat dazed with exhaustion. "I'm scared, and mommy is sleeping. Can I sleep with you guys tonight, pweeze?" "Honey," I begin, as if to offer her a new proposal, "how about I tuck you in and sit with you until you sleep? I think you're still just trying to get used to the new house baby. Would you like that?" It's a question I've asked her almost every night since we've been in our new home. This ritual we've developed plays out the same way, at about the same hour every night, between 9 and 10. "Okay daddy," she says with one of the cutest smiles a little girl can produce.

As I tuck her in, I wait for the words, and here they come. "Daddy?" she begins. "Yes baby?" I follow. "I'm scared, but I know I'll see you again." With a smile, and reciting my lines I say, "of course sweetie, in the morning." "Okay," she goes on, "I just want you to know I'm right here, and I'm not going anywhere. I'll see you again, real soon, just remember that." "I will sweetie, and same to you okay?" I reassure her. A thought strikes me with an open fist, and I'm a little freaked out at how old she sounds when she says that. Don't get me wrong, she's a smart little girl, but this almost sounds like it's coming from a grown woman. I contemplate this for a moment and lay down next to her as I do almost every night, waiting for her to fall asleep, and I doze off.

CHAPTER 3

*I*t was another crazy day at the office, as I say when I've had an

overwhelming day. Overwhelming probably isn't a good word however,

because I'm usually good under pressure, but for a Tuesday it was unusually

busy. Shit, it's only Tuesday and so far this week has turned out to be setting

a personal record for the longest of my life. I'm on my way home but today

I've decided on coming up the back way. I'll take 26 home tonight. I'm not

really in the mood for another reverie to overtake me while I'm on the road,

so I think it's best to postpone going by that building for a bit. Besides,

things have been strange enough with me lately. I just want to get home and

have a normal evening. Then again, my evening will most likely be the

furthest from that. Tamara has given me the silent treatment after last night;

her favorite weapon of choice. I guess it is a little justified. I did kind of lose

it. I'll have to just ride this one out though. I'm not the best with apologies.

As I pull off of the freeway and turn onto Barnes, a thought has just

presented itself, and I guess sometimes the truth hurts. So, maybe I was lying

a little about my happiness. Well wait, I'm happy, just not satisfied, if that

makes sense. I'm not sure what's been going on with me lately but things

have seemed a little, darker, I guess would be a good way to put it; more

gloomy. I've obviously had issues concentrating, and that's not me. It's been

increasingly difficult controlling myself, and making sound judgment calls.

I've never felt this kind of fatigue before either, and the guilt. I've been

feeling very guilty lately. For what I'm not sure, but this odd self-reproach has become as much a normal sensation for me as hunger in the last few weeks. Come to think of it, maybe that's not the best analogy. I haven't really had much of an appetite lately.

On top of all of this Tamara and I have been fighting more since the move and I'm losing my patience very quickly these days. What's worst is we haven't even had sex for about a month. Well, she is very pregnant at the moment; that obviously might have a little to do with it. My sleeping patterns definitely aren't doing me any favors. I haven't been sleeping well at all. Maybe my fucking house is haunted. No, let's be real here. I think I might be depressed. Shaking this concept lose of my mind I notice I've arrived at the gate.

After an awkward evening of staying to ourselves, I'm up late and Tamara and Elli have long been counting sheep. At least Gino still likes me. He's made himself comfortable at my feet. I'm tired now. It's got to be around 1 in the morning and I have to be at work in a few hours. As I rise to turn off the lights and make sure everything is locked up, Gino doesn't abandon his post, but offers me a goodnight stare as he lifts his head to inspect why I've gotten up. "Night Gino." I head up the stairs to my room and quietly make my way to my side of the bed and lay down, making sure to keep my back to her. I immediately shut my eyes and try to block everything else out. I have to get some sleep tonight.

Here we go again, another lovely evening of restlessness. It's not quite insomnia, but I'm just not getting consistent, deep sleep. Something's not right. I think it's the stress. I've had so much on my mind lately. With no other feasible solution offering itself at the moment, ice cream it is. As I get up and take a seat on the edge of my bed, oddly, I notice it's freezing. I blow out in an attempt to draw out a visible cloud of breath, but to no avail. Okay I guess it's not that cold. It vexes me nonetheless that out of nowhere, in mid-July, it's a cold night. It's been so muggy lately that we haven't evened turned off the air conditioner for about the last 3 weeks. Plus, now that I think of it, I don't recall it being a cold evening. I guess that still won't stop me from sacrificing another innocent Ben & Jerry's to the Gods of sleep. That has been my go to solution on many occasions to remedy my wakefulness.

I grab my robe and slip on my slippers. As I walk into the hallway I peak over at Ellis room and notice her sound asleep. Next stop, the kitchen. Proceeding down the steps, each stair produces an unusual creek and crack, noisily announcing my decent. This actually kind of pisses me off; a brand new house and it's already settling as if it's a seasoned veteran. Maybe they were like that before, but I never noticed it. Either way I need to fix that. I won't have my brand new house screaming out aches and pains this early on. Mentally, I add that to the long list of things that I'll get done at some point.

As I reach the foot of the stairwell, my heart almost detonates through my robe at the sound of music and voices in the entertainment room, the man cave. It's at the end of a long hall to the right. Unusually the hallway appears generously extended, and dark, and a red light glows through the bottom of the door to the entertainment room. I squint hard to make out the distance, as it has appeared to continue much further than I remember. What the fuck is going on? I run into the dining room and open up the grandfather clock, barely able to stabilize my shaking hands.

In its belly behind the combination on a safe deposit box rests with anticipation, my Springfield Extreme Duty semi-automatic pistol. It was a little purchase I slipped into the budget without Tamara knowing while I was on a vacation in the Mediterranean. I picked it up in a little city called Karlovac, in Croatia, seemingly for this exact moment. As I spin the combination just as I've practiced so many times, I hear the click of confirmation that I have permission to enter. I swing open the door to the safe. "What the fuck?" I scream. As the panic brutally performs an open heart surgery on me this very instant, tearing me open as the fear dulls the pain, sweat profusely springs from me and I feel every pulsating heartbeat growing intensely, vibrate and throb through every limb; it's empty.

Gino, where is he? I guess he's decided he has better things to do than protect the family that has so lavishly spoiled him with lessons and a raw protein diet suited for the hound of a king. Fucking mut; I'm getting rid of his ass as soon as I find him, if I actually make it out of this. As I'm gripped with a trepidation that has decided that from here I'll proceed like I just ran a marathon, my legs feel extremely heavy and I seem to have lost command over the pace I'd like to maintain. I wobbly make my way to the kitchen for a butcher knife. I guess that's the next best thing. Stumbling through the kitchen I make my way to the hanging cutlery set and quickly scan for the butcher knife in the dim light coming in from our porch lights. Steadying my hands I secure my grip, and slowly turn for the hallway.

As if floating, I get closer to the door somehow, not really conscious of my movements. I notice the music growing louder; some sort of reggae is booming behind the door. There's got to be a few dozen people or more, as I hear a mix of laughter, arguments and singing. I have a second thought about entering now, and decide on a thought that for some reason hasn't presented itself until now, the police. Wait, they should have been here by now anyway. My home security system automatically notifies them in the event of a break in. Regardless of my indecisiveness, now it appears that I have no choice in the matter. I don't even feel my body at this point and the door to the entertainment room has secured a noose around my waist that pulls me closer without regard for my granting it. I brace a little as the pace that I travel increases the closer I get to the door and I'm about to slam right into it, or through it.

All of the sudden it swings open, and a group of people scream and cheer at the sight of my entry. "We've been waiting on you baby?" I look over and an attractive blond with a long tee shirt and no pants on is rubbing my arm. As I examine the room, there's a bed of syringes blanketing the floor and I notice that my entire man cave has been remodeled and refurnished. There's a thick haze about the room, but I can slightly make out two people having sex on a sofa, a group of people passing around a bong, others taking turns shooting up, still others walking around in and out of the fog that surrounds different pockets of the room, and a few staring at me. Just then I feel the sharp pinch of a needle thrust into my arm, and the blonde's face suddenly appears out of the fog directly in front of mine. With her this close to me, I can make out the smeared lipstick on her face, her dilated pupils under baggy, drugged lids, the hair of a messy mop on top of her head. "Here's your medicine baby," she says, as she delivers the needle deeper into my arm. I squint and shut my eyes as it excavates further.

When I open my eyes I'm laying on the floor in my room next to my bed in the position that I originally assumed when I went to bed tonight. It's quiet. I explode into a kneeling position over my side of the bed and see Tamara sleeping soundly in the same spot she was when I closed my eyes to sleep. My side of the bed is soaked with sweat. I'm too scared to get up and go make sure everything is back to normal, so I stay, and just stare off into the room. Just then my alarm goes off, and at its declaration I slap it with a startled reflex; 5 in the morning. My head automatically slumps heavily down into my hands. I'm losing my mind. I grab my cell phone and search the list of contacts. Dr. Hillman, it's time we meet again. He's my therapist. I haven't been with him for too long, but we hit it off immediately and I respect and admire the work he does. Someone told me to look him up when I got to Portland. I can't take this anymore.

CHAPTER 4

*F*rom the tone of your voice I could tell this was serious Seth," he

begins as he suddenly appears in the waiting room, revealed behind a swung open door leading back to his office. "I very much appreciate you rearranging your schedule for me Ian," I reply as I rise to follow. He offers me his hand and I grab it firmly and shake, then continue, "I know you're a busy man, and very loyal to your patients," secretly thinking to myself the exception was most likely only made due to my status. I've been one of his best, meaning high paying, clients as of late. I get full coverage for these visits with my insurance; one of the perks of being an anesthesiologist. Who knows, maybe he has genuinely taken a liking to me and really cares so much for my well-being; just me out of the hundreds of patients he sees. "I do these things for people I like," he says in a whisper, leaning in to conceal his supposed partiality.

"Right this way," he says as if this is our first encounter; always the very professional Mr. Hillman. "So tell me about what's been going on lately Seth," he prompts me, putting on his therapist face. "Well Ian, where do I start?" I say with a chuckle as I investigate my thoughts. "Ever since the move things have kind of gone downhill. I've been, unusually stressed, irritable, and restless. I'm not quite experiencing insomnia, but I'm definitely having issues sleeping, and every now and then when I do get enough sleep, I oversleep, and feel even more drained when I wake." As I verbalize these things aloud, I can feel the frustration forming a lump in my stomach and throat simultaneously, and I briefly look away and inhale enormously to try and relieve the discomfort.

Looking back at him, I go on, "Now usually I'm a really," I stop short of saying cocky, and reassess my words, "confident person, you know, but lately I've felt kind of hopeless. I've kind of lost interest in all of the things I used to have a healthy luster for, even sex, so I know something is really wrong" I throw out, in an attempt to liven the Dr. up a bit. There's a concerned look that he's displaying, and its depth is becoming a little too much for me to bear at the moment. So the attempted joke may have been a little more for me than him. He doesn't laugh at the jest, but I do however coax a smile out of his unsettled countenance. "I've been really fatigued," I continue, "I've even had a lot of digestive issues and upset stomach lately, that is, after the meals I actually force myself to get down. I don't know, the list can go on." With that I pause for his feedback.

Getting the hint, he takes the floor. He inhales, deeply exhales in thought, and then leans back in his chair, staring intensely into my gaze. "Let me ask you this, have these feelings been consistent, for long periods?" he asks. "I'd say I've really noticed them about the last couple of weeks," I reply. "Have you had any thoughts of suicide or have tried to attempt suicide. Seth I need you to be honest," he pitches at me. "What, no!" I respond, "Gosh no." "Okay," he replies a little more relaxed, "That's good. Well Seth, from what I've heard you're exhibiting all of the classic signs of depression." With his words, I feel a weird comfort in the revelation because this was something I was already presuming. I'm just relieved he didn't think it was something more serious, not that this isn't serious enough. "I kind of suspected that," I confirm.

"The good news is," he starts with a new, revitalized tone; "I think I have a very, very effective solution for you." "What kind of meds do you think I'll need?" I automatically draw out the idea, so used to this approach in the hospital environment I thrive in. "Meds?" he repeats as his brows rise and furrow the skin above them. "I have a," he pauses in his thought and reflects for a moment, "better solution in mind Seth." With this, he gets up and goes over to a big easel looking notepad and grabs a sharpie. He quickly turns and directs a sharp, scrutinizing look my way, and proclaims, "Our session is over." As a dumfounded look invites itself onto my face, he turns his back on me and faces the board.

"However," he goes on, "that doesn't mean we're finished here. Seth, I like you. I appreciate anyone who undergoes a pursuit to save thousands of people throughout their career, someone who, comforts those in times of their most intense and overwhelming moments. We need more people like you. I don't mind doing favors for those of you, who like me, through our careers can benefit the lives of so many, and I want to speak with you now, as a friend, not a therapist. I want to leave behind for a moment, the limits of the ethical principles of psychologists and codes of conduct we must adhere to as therapists. So, like I said, the session is over, but I want to talk to you man-to-man, friend-to-friend. I sincerely believe it is in your best interest.

He lifts the sharpie to the paper and begins drawing. It looks like some sort of graph or table. He's drawn a large line going up and slightly toward the middle of the paper, where he's written 75,000. Next to this he draws a strait, horizontal line across the page, and then a line heading down as it travels further right toward the edge of the paper. Vertically, to the left of the graph he writes the word happiness, and at the bottom, income. I see where he's going.

He sets down the sharpie and turns to face me once again. "Can money buy us happiness?" he simply poses the question. "Truthfully," he starts in, "there's a lot of conflicting data behind the research of this question. Though, many studies appear to produce the same answer; 75,000." He points to the number, then goes on, "the lower a person's annual income falls below that benchmark, in America, the more unhappy he or she tends to feel. That number is really debatable. The biggest point here is that, it seems, once our basic needs and necessities are comfortably met, and then some, our happiness does in fact appear to improve.

Then interestingly, above a certain income, for our sake the number is 75,000, the higher we get above that point our happiness levels out, and money is no longer the prime influence of our happiness. What's even more interesting about these studies, as you can see, is that they all reflect that after a certain point as our income increases further, the potential for our happiness tends to decline, further suggesting that in fact, money may cause just the opposite of happiness. This is what I believe you are experiencing.

Now, the question that these studies have all failed to answer here is, what is the root of this effect?" he says, as he directs his finger to the point on the graph where the line connecting to the horizontal line across the page starts heading down. He pauses, and looks into my eyes inquisitively, awaiting my response. Feeling inclined to answer but not really having a solid comprehension of one, I suggest, "I don't know, Ian." I produce a strained smile to show my submission in the failure to yield a proper response, but he doesn't bite, and holds his ground in silence. "Maybe," I go on, "maybe, maybe it's the fact that, after they've accumulated so much they feel that there is nothing else to work toward? Maybe they lose their passion for life a bit." My response came out posed more as a question than an answer. I was definitely reaching for anything convincing.

"Seth," he finally initiates, "you were close my friend. You had part of the word." After another brief pause he says, "compassion. Now realize, this is purely my opinion, but so far, it's been the most valid conclusion I've heard thus far. Now first off, I don't want this to be a religious conversation. I don't want it to sound that way, but I naturally, being a spiritual person myself, draw much of my inspiration for any undertaking in my life from a wealth of religions inspiration. Furthermore, I truly believe that you don't need religion to have morals. If you can't determine wrong from right then you lack empathy, not religion.

Compassion," he continues. "In his book, Toward a True Kinship of Faiths, the great Dalai Lama explains compassion as, 'the natural capacity of the human heart to feel concern for and connection with another being.' He goes on to note that this 'constitutes a basic aspect of our nature shared by all human beings,' that, 'there is not an iota of difference between a believer and a nonbeliever, nor between people of one race or another. All ethical teachings, whether religious or nonreligious, aim to nurture this innate and precious quality, to develop it and to perfect it.' You see Seth; this is precisely the reason for this decrease in happiness as one accumulates an income that comes to represent excess. How can you truly be happy while so many others are suffering, poor, sick, slowly dying for lack of health care, illiterate and in poverty, while you have such an excess of abundance, if, you lack compassion?

Compassion transcends religion. However, on the subject of religion, why does it even exist? I believe that after enough soul searching, after enough investigating and philosophizing, the one common denominator of every religion points to the attainment of happiness, weather it is ultimately in this life, or the next, and with that said Seth, there's no coincidence why compassion is highlighted as a major concept and component to fostering this happiness, in every religion; they all reference compassion Seth, every single one. You can find it in the Mahabharata in 5:1517 in Hinduism, in the Hillel, in the Talmud for the Sabbath 31a in Judaism, the Dadisten-I-dinik 94:5 in Zoroastrianism, the Udanavarga 5:20 in Buddhism. Jainism speaks of it in the Sutrakritanga 1.11:33. In Daoism, it is referenced in the Tai-Shang Kan-ying P'ien, in Confucianism in the Analects 12:2, amongst Christian text in Matthew 7:12 and in Islam, in the Hadith of al-Nawawi 13. There is absolutely no denying this correlation. Compassion is precisely the blueprint for happiness."

His words pierce right through the heart of me, because I know he speaks the truth. It absolutely makes sense. Oddly, the power of their influence invokes a tremendous sense of guilt, and at the same time offers me an out, an opportunity to dig myself out of the enormous, dreary cavern of dejection, confusion and sorrow that I've stumbled into as of late. Perhaps reading and interpreting the shame that has peered through my face, even though I'm trying to maintain a temperate expression, he breaks into my self pity with, "I have a suggestion for you Seth; well, actually a couple. First off, read that book," he offers with a smile.

"Secondly," he continues, "why don't you try it out? Help somebody, and not as a commitment to your career as you do through your profession; not that kind of help. On your own time, under your own influence, help somebody. Take the time to relate to somebody who is less fortunate and try to really understand their position in life, and see if there is anything you can do to alleviate any of it. Humanitarianism and compassion are one in the same. Now that you've conquered the world financially; now that you are part of that upper class, 2 percent of the population that many people will never have the opportunity to reach, there's one thing left that you haven't conquered, and that's compassion. You owe it to yourself to give it a try. I want to see you in a week so we can assess the outcome and see if it has helped you in any way. I'll see you next Wednesday; same time?" Out of my shame I muster a quiet and restrained, "that should work." "Wednesday it is," he immediately fires back, with a smile so large I feel like it might get stuck that way.

"Ian," I squeak in a similar fashion as Elli would to me. "Yes Seth," he replies, maintaining his smile. "I want to thank you, very much. This might be the most I've ever gotten out of one of our sessions, and I truly have taken what you've said to heart, truly. There is just, one more thing." "Okay," he assures me. "There's some stuff I haven't told you yet," I confirm. Waiting for me to continue his smile slowly retreats as the concern that he expressed before slowly trades its place. I start in, "I've been having some really weird, visions and dreams lately. I guess you could call them hallucinations; weird headaches. I really don't get headaches much but lately they've been almost daily." With a confused look, he shifts a little and asks, "any nausea and vomiting?" "Not really, well, maybe a little nausea here and there," I confirm. "What about memory loss, weakness, difficulty walking or loss of balance?" In a louder tone and faster pace he continues, "visual changes, problems with speech and language?" "Woah, woah," I cut him off. "Slow down a little doc. Actually, yes, I've experienced all of those things lately," I say.

With that, he for a split second flashes a face of sorrow in my direction, and then is quickly cognicent to wipe it clear and replace it with one of urgency. "I've heard things like this before Seth, and this could be serious." My heart flutters in response to his discernment. "Well couldn't it just be exhaustion?" I propose. "It could be, but I'd rather be safe than sorry, as always Seth," he responds. "I want you to go see your primary physician, tomorrow!" "Tomorrow?" I ask, "I'll have to," "Seth," he cuts me off, "come on, don't give me that. You work at a hospital. This could be serious. I'm sure you could figure something out. Okay, promise me you'll do it as soon as possible, and I still want to see you in a week." With a growing sense of panic making itself comfortable in my body, I try to persuade, "I'll see what I can do okay Ian, and I'll see you next Wednesday." As I approach the door, I hear, "Oh, here you go Seth, I have something for you to read, take this."

I grab the packet he's provided me and once again thank him. "See you next Wednesday," I say, and make my exit. On my way out to the car I quickly scan over bits and pieces of this reading he's provided me. 'Patients with nervous system tumors often develop early changes in their cognitive abilities.' Tumors? The thought releases a surge of uneasy excitement as I finally piece together the urgency that my therapist exhibited to me moments ago for me to go get checked out. So he thinks I may have a tumor, and the more I read, so do I. 'These changes include difficulties remembering things, changes in personality or mood, lack of initiative, and also poor judgment. Depending on where the tumor is located, a person may have trouble reading, writing or difficulties speaking. Furthermore, it may be very difficult for some folks to engage in abstract reasoning. Many people with brain tumors suffer from sleep disorders, periodic restlessness and are unable to concentrate;' Fuck.

I get into my car and prepare for the road, but again, I'm drawn back to this article. 'Specific neurological abnormalities caused by brain tumors vary from patient to patient.' I flip the page. 'When the areas of the brain responsible for sensing the environment, called the sensory structures, are damaged by a tumor, the patient may feel tingling, numbness, or other odd sensations.' I flip again. 'Some patients experience not being able to recognize parts of their environment. For example, if the tumor is in the temporal lobe of the brain, a person may see hallucinations or experience other unusual perceptions.' I need to get in, tomorrow.

CHAPTER 5

Well, it's my turn to play the patient. They made special arrangements for me by request of Mr. Hillman. He actually called on my behalf and after I confirmed his plea, arrangements were made for me to get in today. I was told this morning that I was presenting symptoms suggestive of a brain tumor, which made for an extremely long Thursday as my anticipation for the next step intruded my thoughts, and performance, the rest of the day. After a thorough history and physical examination, radiology imaging is the next task at hand.

Following my MRI I was told the results would be interpreted this evening and that I would be notified of the results tomorrow. If something shows, there may have to be some further imaging studies to determine if the mass in in fact a tumor as opposed to other causes such as infection, and if it is a tumor, what type. The next step would be an MR spectroscopy. These allow the physician to learn more about the contents of the mass and helps them determine what the mass is. This is important, I was told, because it allows the doctor to map the brain and helps the doctor know which areas to avoid during surgery if the tumor is close to a portion of the brain, say, which is critical for movement or speech. I have an intuition, due to the recent events at my home, that I very well may be screwed here, but I'm trying to stay positive.

On my way home I try to concoct a plan of how I'll relay all of this to Tamara without freaking her out. The last thing I need is for her to get stressed and overly anxious, especially this close to delivery. On top of that, if she freaks out, I freak out even more. She tends to have that effect on me. As I'm envisioning the scenario in my mind like the practicing of an upcoming play I'm the main character of, I snap out of my fancy just in time to see him. There's a transient that sits right where the road to my neighborhood connects to Barnes road, on that corner. I've seen him many a days; have made eye contact with him a time or two, but have never actually interacted with him. Why would I have? Anyhow, now's my chance. I swerve quickly to pull onto the side of the road right by where his sits on the corner, and through my review I notice his head whip around in a startled, instinctive spontaneity, and he jumps to his feet. He probably thought I was going to get out and kick his ass or something. I can't blame him. I did suddenly pull a very wild and abrupt jerk to the side of the road just past where he sat.

I turn off the car and glance at him once more in the rearview. This time I can see him stopped, and peering into my car to try and make out who in the world it might be. I open the door, and turn toward him with my hands up as if he has the scope of a rifle bearing down on me. "It's okay," I assure him as I approach. "Man, I thought you were undercover or something," he says in raspy tone. I immediately get a whiff of weeks old clothes and body odor. "No, not me," I assure him once more, hoping to calm him down a little. "Well what the fuck was that then?" he asks, with the raise of a single brow.

"Well," I stop and look down, placing my hands upon my hips and trying to figure out what exactly it is I am doing here, "good question," I reply with a grin that strains to manifest. "I want to, talk to you, if you don't mind." "Talk to me?" he repeats my question. "What are you crazy?" he follows. "Actually, yes," I respond, this time not laughing but producing a hearty guffaw from him. "So what, is this like a project for school or something?"

he goes on, attempting it seems, to build some rapport. "You actually believe I'm a broke college student, at the ripe old age of 47, living here?" I say, as I point over my shoulder in the direction of my neighborhood. "You never know," he says, giving me a joking sarcasm. "No actually these days you really never know," he says, with a stern intensity. "I guess you're right," I agree, "but it would be a long shot." "Wait," he goes on, "I've seen you before."

"Yeah, I'm sure you have," I reply. "No I have," he fires back enthusiastically. "You're one of the only ones around here who's actually smiled at me, much less made eye contact with me," he informs. "You're not like the others around here. You don't belong here." At that, I give him a confused gander, missing the intention behind the statement. In response to the confusion I wear, he quickly changes the subject, "but you know what? You haven't given me any money either," he throws my way. As the words escape his mouth, I look down attempting to somehow avoid their reality. Then I feel a swat on my shoulder, "hey, it's okay," he says in a loud tone. "A smile is as good as gold to me. Those things are rare around here."

So you want to get to know me huh?" he asks, well, kind of repeats, as he heads back over to the corner to sit, I assume expecting me to follow. I follow him over and take a seat next to him, letting my legs relax comfortably on the curb. As I lean back and brace myself with my hands behind my back, I notice that he and I are immediately victims of glares intent on full injury from the drivers moving swiftly by, some stopping at the corner offering even longer scowls. "So, you're homeless," I begin, quickly realizing that I've obviously failed to mask the fact that apparently, I'm an amateur to something like this, and have just began the conversation on somewhat of an awkward note.

"Well no shit Sherlock," he offers me, giving me an 'are you serious' dagger through the side of my face with his look. With a laugh, I go on,

"Why here?" "Why here?" he reflects aloud in thought. "Well, I'm from here. I'm comfortable with it I guess. I know the good spots, the bad spots, and everywhere in between. "Yeah," I cut in, "but with the rain, and the cold, I mean this time of year isn't too bad, but wouldn't it be easier in say, Arizona or California or something?" "Well, maybe in some ways, but when you're homeless there's more things to consider than just the weather," he follows. "Like I said. I know the area. It's been my home since I was a kid. I know where I can actually pull in some cash. Plus, it's either save up enough money for a bus ticket to a place I'm a complete stranger to, and get lost somewhere new, starving, or just stay put," he says in deep thought. "I see," I reply.

In a brief silence, as I search for what to say next, I see him look over at me in my peripheral. As I turn to meet his gaze, he offers a sincere, "So what do you want, my story?" As I search myself for confirmation of that being why I'm here, I don't answer quite yet, and I hear, "yeah, well, believe it or not none of us are born this way okay? It can happen to anyone. That's why I sit here man; as a constant reminder that homelessness is not always about our decisions. Sometimes it's simply about circumstance. Sometimes, things that are out of our control can spiral, into, into, a bottomless dungeon of hurt and isolation, where the end result is what you see."

He looks down, then looks back up, but not at me. "Without the proper, support, and guidance," he goes on, "this is the future of many, good people. The privileged few, you know, them," he says as he points in the direction I did when I referenced my home before, "they automatically take the stance to liken our stories merely to us being screw ups; lazy, unmotivated scum that live off of the rest of society." He pauses, and in the absence of his voice, I offer, "you know, you sound pretty intelligent, for, for." I stop short of the proper finish. He looks away and says, "for a bum?" attempting to finish my thought. "It's okay," he goes on. "Is that enough for you? You can leave now. Besides, I don't do stories. You wouldn't believe mine anyway."

Again, as I've been most of the conversation, I'm still desperately combing my vocabulary for the most appropriate words to fill the void of silence I supply. "No, that's not enough," I say, just figuring that honesty might be the best remedy in this situation.

"Not enough?" he replies. "Well how about since I have you here, let me take this opportunity to get to know you a little," he says a little angrily, possibly in preparation to ridicule the reluctant stranger who seems too confused to offer any wisdom or help. "Why did you really pull over today?" he inquires. "Well, wait, what's your name?" I ask, trying to establish some sort of common ground. "You can call me Mickey. People used to call me Mickey because I have big ears." He stops, finally offering me a smile, and while shaking his head, looks back at the ground and then off in the distance and says, "but it doesn't bother me anymore." "Well Mickey," I reply, offering him my hand, "I'm Seth. It's nice to meet you." "Yeah," he says, not acknowledging my hand for a moment, then finally slowly offering his in return, replies, "you too."

"So why did I pull over?" I say, feeling a little more, acquainted. "Well, honestly Mickey, I've been having a hard time lately, and I," "Wait," he cuts me off, "you live here, and you're having a hard time?" he retorts with a somewhat cynical laugh. In response to my blank stare, possibly finally recognizing my sincerity at attempting to, befriend him, he hesitatingly says, "Look, I'm sorry. This is just a little strange for me, and I obviously have some pent up, feelings, that haven't been dealt with. Go on." "Mickey," I start back, "believe it or not, I understand, and it's fine, I don't blame you. Like I said, I've been having some, issues lately, and somebody suggested that this could help me." "Oh, is this like a charity thing or something?" he questions. "No, no," I assert. "Issues, what are you depressed or something?" he replies. "You could say that," I say, looking off into my own cloud of reflection.

"So talking to me could help huh? Well, I won't give you my story, that doesn't really matter now, but I will give you a taste of my life. How about that?" he proposes. I nod in approval. "I've been living like this for about 2 years now," he begins. I never would have imagined I'd be homeless, but," he abruptly halts, attempting already to fight back a welling pool of tears. "As they say," he spits out, his voice cracking like a boy who just hit puberty, "shit happens." He swipes at his eyes with a sleeve, and puts a hand over his bowing head and shields his face from my gaze. I can only imagine what must have happened, something very tragic it appears, but I don't ask.

"The longer my life goes on like this I feel like I might never get back on my feet again. I've tried to find a job, but when you show up to ask for an application, and you don't look even halfway presentable, you get no chance. Then when you have to explain to them that you can't leave an address or phone number because you don't have one, everyone in the store dismisses you as trash." He pauses, trying to regain some composure and muster enough control to go on. "Most times," he presses forward, "I don't have enough money for a flophouse downtown so I sleep in the park or on one of the benches in front of a building." As he speaks, some imaginary force has taken a knife that has begun to slowly make an incision into my chest, up my throat and through me ear. I feel a sour lump form in my throat that too, is ready to open a floodgate of tears on my face.

"Usually I have to start my day at 5 or 6 in the morning when the security guards for the office buildings come and run me off of the benches, or if the morning joggers come running through the park. This shit all feels so humiliating, so humiliating. I never would have thought I'd be panhandling to survive. There's something about it that feels less than human. One day, a guy walked past me and said some of the most hurtful and nasty things anyone has ever said to me, but the thing that hurt me the most was when he called me a bum." Again, he wipes his face dry and looks down to conceal the watersheds that have become his eyes. "I'm not a bum," he says, as he looks up and into my eyes, sharing his tears as I feel them coming down my cheeks. "I'm a human being," he continues. "You want to know what I did? I just looked at him and said god bless you, and he walked off. Later that day the same man came back and said he had been having a bad day and asked if I'd accept his apology. That was one of the first times I ever felt like maybe there are people out there who do care.

Compassion; again the word rings in my ears from some invisible source in my conscience. "So why are you not happy?" he asks, with a sniffle. "Honestly Mickey," I begin, "I'm still trying to figure that out, but I think I'm starting to." "I mean, you have the American Dream right up the road here," he says, pointing once more toward my neighborhood. "You have the pursuit of happiness, right? Well, let me tell you about the American Dream I see. I see a nation, nurturing each generation to be independent, and isolated. Now we have social networking instead of actually building and fostering relationships with effort and sincerity. Now it's easier than ever to stay isolated and independent. I see people so obsessed and worried about their status that they work themselves to death, neglect their families, and spend more time in the workplace than at home.

These doctors and professors and attorneys, who have children that they barely even raise; their only form of investment in those children amounts only to financial security." As he goes on I can't help but realize how brilliant and articulate he actually is, surprisingly, weather I agree with him or not. Then what checks my chin and forces me to assess my own integrity, is the fact that based on his, situation, and appearance, I've prejudged him unfairly. "These kids," he goes on, "lack support, and parenting, and grow up without a true sense of themselves. They lack the confidence necessary to survive in this world. Obviously this is a simple reality for those children of families that thrive in the poverty and desolation of the majority of society. In either scenario, many of these children turn to drugs and sex, and anything else that can give them a false sense of the security they've never experienced in the one place it should have begun, home.

I see an American Dream that leads the world in obesity and heart disease, overworked motherfuckers, and stress levels through the roof, you know? Who the fuck wants that? Then people wonder why there's so many unhappy people in our country, a country where, kids get picked on and bullied because there's no compassion." As soon as the word leaves his lips, I get a cold chill of actuality that, now I can't deny, something is trying to reach me, and this word, compassion, has undeniably been the weapon of choice. "Then," he continues, "when that kid gets old enough to comprehend a mass shooting or a bombing, he turns on anybody in his path in the wake of his vengeance. It's crazy man. Oh, and don't even get me started on capitalism!

It's all a big business, this country, and if you're not playing, you'll lose your monopoly piece forever, and the game continues without you. The holidays are the worst for me. So many people scurrying about, stressed and depressed, anxious about not having enough for the family, when there's people right here in there own backyard who spend the holidays, cold, and alone. There's people in other countries who don't have fucking water for god's sake, and we have Thanksgiving, and Easter Sunday, where we indulge in the worlds biggest fest of gluttony. Plus, I mean look at all of the wars and controversy we've been involved in. We lack compassion for anything un-American, bottom line; other cultures, other races, other forms of government. That's not happiness. That's a recipe for disaster. That's America.

It's nothing against you man, we're just missing something here." "Compassion," I hear myself say without even contemplating it. "Exactly," he concurs. "The best and most beautiful things cannot be seen or even touched, they must be felt with the heart; Helen Keller said that," he informs me. "I read that once," he continues, "and realized that, I can be happy in any situation, as long as I have compassion. Once we learn that, once everyone learns that, I believe we can have the country that our forefathers envisioned; one nation, under god, indivisible, with Liberty and Justice for all. Fucking America," he says as he looks away and his voice trails off with his gaze.

Lost in my own contemplation, ushered in by his view of America, I finally break our shared, inner scrutinization with, "well, is there anything I can do to help you." He slowly turns to me, and with a wholehearted response, replies, "yeah, actually you can. You can find me a lady with a nice rear to begin with," as he lets out a hearty laugh, and I reflexively join. "No," he says as his laughter suddenly ceases, "that's not what I need. I've already had my love." I notice at this he begins to again, get choked up and stares away from me, his face avoiding my line of sight. "I had two loves, the loves of my life, and I was the happiest man in the world, until they were taken from me about 2 years ago." With his head hanging low, I can see a steady drip of tears forming a puddle in between his legs. I can feel the intense amount of pain he is in as if our bodies were connected by some force of nature, but again, I don't ask. "That's why I'm here." Again, we share a brief silence, as I internalize different scenarios of what could have been his experience, until it is broken by him chiming in, "I don't want your money.

How about this? Every time you get the opportunity, show someone compassion. Maybe the next guy won't end up like me. That thought alone is help enough," he says, and then braces himself in a comfortable position, signaling that he has spoken. "You know, you're one of the smartest people I've ever met," I say, trying to encourage him a bit, "and I think you'll be okay, I really do. I'm very happy we met, and talked." "I'm glad we met too," he insists, "and I hope I helped you with, whatever it is you're going through. Like I said, you're better than them, and you don't belong here.

That's why I gave you up. I always knew you would be something, something special, but you couldn't be something special here. I hope you forgive me for giving you up, but more than that, I hope you will one day understand why." Startled at his response, not because of him, but because I once more appear to be, hallucinating, or something, I shake that comment free of my mindset and reach for my wallet.

As I reveal two hundred dollar bills I hear, "oh no man, I can't." "Please," I quickly negotiate. "You said you hope you helped me, well this will. This is more for me than you. Take it, please; Merry Christmas." "In July?" he jokingly questions, appearing all of the sudden invigorated at the thought of becoming 200 dollars richer. "In July," I reply with a large smile intent on taking over my face. "That's it," he says, "compassion; and you already look like you're doing better!" "I feel better," I assure him as he takes the money. "We'll speak again soon," I say, hoping inside that we actually will. "I hope so," he says. As I turn and walk back to my car, he says, "Merry Christmas," and I smile back and wave; compassion.

CHAPTER 6

*T*he sun is magnificently bright this Friday morning. Our master

bedroom faces the east and usually catches the rising sun in the morning. This morning it appears that Tamara is off to an early start, and has apparently wanted me to do the same. She's slid the curtains open, revealing a dazzling burst of sunshine, apparent to me even through the closed lids of my eyes. That's what woke me up. This was supposed to be a late day for me. I was going to see my doctor at 9 a.m. this morning for the results, and then go into work. It's 7:30 and I guess it was actually a good thing she invited the sun to peak through. I'm not sure I even set my alarm. That could have been bad.

I rise and slide my feet over the side of the bed. I take a moment to stretch, and hear the song of birds singing right outside of my window. I go to it and look out, investigating the flowers in bloom and notice a squirrel, slowly making its way through the yard, stopping here and there to sift through the grass for stashed away goodies. Today seems different, in a good way. I'm noticing little things that I used to pay no mind to, and it actually makes a sense of appreciation I've never realized before this, relevant, in a very pleasant way. I go downstairs and sit on the loveseat in our main family room. It's kind of odd; everyone is gone, including Rosie and the dog. Maybe they're out grocery shopping and didn't want to wake me. I don't know.

I take a sip of the water that I stopped and got myself while making my way to the family room, and set it down to take a moment to sort through my day while I relax. I close my eyes and rest my head back on the sofa. Flash!

A bright light beams across my eyes and I open them to see a ceiling, as if I was lying on some sort of bed. I notice lights to the sides of me and begin to scan the room. I'm strapped down to the bed and feel poked and prodded, and then I hear voices. Flash! Just then I come out of it, and I look around again out at the peaceful morning I had just been experiencing seconds before. As I squint and rub my eyes, Flash! When I open them this time, I'm in the same position, and I hear a man's voice call out, "hypoxic-anoxic injury." In another flash I'm sitting back in my family room. Right away, another flash sends me back to this room, a hospital room I discern, and I hear the same voice again, "pinpoint pupils is a sign. We have another one." This time, a flash sends a shockwave through my body that launches me back against the cushion of the loveseat.

At that moment the phone rings and that too, produces a launch of my body in response to the startling I received from the announcement of our home phone. This time however, I launch into a seated position on my bed. I look over and notice Tamara still resting peacefully on her side of the bed, and immediately I look over at my alarm clock; 7:30 a.m. I quickly reach for my cell phone; Friday, July 13th. My cell phone begins to buzz in my hand, comfortably vibrating it. It's the Chief of Anesthesiology. For some reason I'm too, afraid, to answer. A voicemail; I better check it. "Seth, go ahead and take the day off okay. We have enough staff for today," Dr. Adams voice plays back. After a pause, he finishes with, "Have a good weekend Seth, and I wish you the best Seth."

My adrenal glands go into overdrive at the completion of the message. I quickly look over at my wife, who is completely oblivious to all of this, and realize I better slither quietly out of bed and get ready and gone before she gets up. I'd like to keep it that way for the time being. My appointment is at 9. I'm going to show up early. I need some time to think.

As I sit in the waiting room after I have checked in, I can't help but let my thoughts gravitate toward the worst possible scenarios. Then I start thinking of things like, how bad is it? What stage? How much longer will I have? My family will be fine, at least financially, but who's going to be there for all of the birthdays, the birth of my son, proms, games, weddings? I can feel the tears begin to infiltrate my eyes, so I grab a magazine and shuttle my face between the pages. The others in the room must think this is the greatest article in the very used magazines offered to us. Truthfully, I'm not sure what I'm going to hear, so maybe I should stop working myself up, but at this point I can hardly help it.

"Seth McGiness," I hear myself summoned. When I enter the office, my primary, Dr. Joseph Carlisle, is already sitting in the room. The nurse leaves without a word and shuts the door behind her. In the silence that follows, I can't contain my concern any longer, and I blurt, "so?" "Seth," he begins in a somber note, "please, take a seat." As I slowly force my body to move, overcoming the nervousness building in anticipation, I finally make it to the hospital bed, and slowly lower my body to a seated position as if I were catching its lifeless weight and bracing for a soft landing. He slides down his glasses, produces a stern gaze, and begins, "Seth, we found something." Okay, I think, short and sweet; so what does that mean? I'm pretty familiar with the generalities of doctors, so I wait for more without working myself up further for no apparent reason.

"Imaging of tumor blood flow with the use of perfusion MRI may give us more insight into the lesion, and even measuring tumor metabolite concentration with MR spectroscopy may add additional value to a standard MRI in the diagnosis of the tumor." "So a tumor is what we're dealing with here?" I cut in. "Correct," he responds immediately. "However, stereotactic biopsy is still the gold standard to properly diagnose what exactly it is we're dealing with." At this, the concern begins to regain strength, but still, I wait for more. "Stereotactic biopsy is a procedure where a very thin needle is inserted into the brain to extract a small piece of the tissue to examine under a microscope.

The goal is to properly diagnose the abnormality seen on the MRI. You see, MRIs are very effective for showing parts of the brain that are abnormal, yet they can't tell us with 100 percent certainty what an abnormality represents. Furthermore, even being certain that this is a tumor; it does not provide us with supplementary information, such as whether it is cancerous or benign. The image of your MRI will be imported into a computer system that will provide us with a 3-dimensional image of your brain and our biopsy target while we are in the operating room. This image, along with a biopsy guidance arm, is used to guide our needle safely into the tumor target."

He hesitates, surely in response to my blank stare, possibly representing also one of low blood sugar, as I feel a stark coolness slowly exchange itself for the natural warmth of my skin. "Seth," he goes on, "as your doctor, it's very important that I notify you of exactly what is going on, and the proper steps necessary from here on out." "I know, I know," I snap back forcefully, "I'm a doctor myself, remember?" Suddenly realizing how that came out, I try to retract and apologize, "I'm sorry. This is just, all a bit to take in at once," I say, trying to contain the nausea that has made itself known. "I understand Seth," he informs me.

"The success rate for obtaining a definitive diagnosis using this method," he goes on in his somewhat bland, nonchalant conveyance "is 95 percent, and is highest for tumors. The risks, well the biggest risk is bleeding in the tumor and brain from the biopsy needle. Bleeding can cause anything from a mild headache up to a stroke, coma, or possibly even death. Now before that gets you too worked up, the risk of bleeding following biopsy is around 5 percent and the risk of mortality is around 1 percent. Additional risks can include mild headache from the biopsy site, infection, and seizures. As you know

Seth, we do everything we can, and take every precaution in our power to minimize risk. Also, procedure is to keep everyone overnight in the hospital for observation at the completion of surgery."

Overnight? Overnight; the concept invokes an anxiety that decides to cloud my mind and repeat itself rhythmically. I guess my idea of concealing all of this from Tamara has just come to an abrupt termination. Either way I'm screwed. I can't just not show up at home one evening; that would never go over well, and I could never lie to her about the true basis of an overnight hospital stay. I may be a self-centered, greedy bastard, but one thing I'm not is dishonest, especially to my wife, regardless of our dynamic at the time. The next concern which rears its unyielding head right through my thoughts is, how will I possibly explain it to her in a way that won't add more tension and strain on an already heated pressure pot of an existence?

"How long will I be in the hospital, just overnight?" I inquire in a shaky inflection. "Just overnight," he assures me. "We'll send you home, after, we discuss the results of your biopsy." A tremendous terror shreds apart any comfort I may have still possessed, and I slump weakly in my seated position as if my spine has completely given up all ability to stabilize. "Oh, you know what?" I hear. "I'm sorry, the results won't be processed and interpreted until 48 hours after the biopsy. So, we'll talk Sunday." "Come on doc, you're killing me," I relay, as my emotions continue on the biggest roller coaster ride in the theme park that is my imagination.

"I apologize Seth," he responds with a chuckle. Immediately after he expels his apology, he switches back to his unbending, informative air. "Would you like to call your wife and let her know?" "What do you mean?" I ask, a little confused. Just then I put together what he's just informed me of, and do the math. He said the results would be available on Sunday, 48 hours after the biopsy, which would mean that he was intending the biopsy be done today, right now! "Seth this is serious," he informs. "As soon as I had the results back from the MRI, knowing that we had an appointment today, I made room to have the biopsy scheduled. We need to get a move on this, immediately." I pause in an intense reflection, with my thoughts all competing for a clear view in my mind. After what seemed minutes, I respond, "I better call her."

CHAPTER 7

*T*he procedure went smoothly, and after a very heavily sedated night's

sleep, I wait patiently for them to inform me that I can depart. My head

throbs under the dressing they've wrapped around it, but other than that, I'm

pretty comfortable. "Seth," I hear a call from the door. It's not my surgeon

or my doctor, but a nurse, peaking her head through the opening, "you

awake?"

"Yes I am," I call back. Just then, she reveals herself, and motions to

somebody behind her to follow. A very small woman, hunched over in old

age and moving slowly with her cane appears, and begins a trek in my

direction. It seems to take several minutes before they reach my bed, and

when they do, she places a wrinkly hand on my forearm, and slowly lifts her

head as if it weighed a few tons, and she is using an imaginary crane to do so.

Finally, her eyes meet mine. The nurse is standing closely by. "Hello Seth,"

she begins in a shaky, quiet voice, strained through aged vocal cords. "My

name is Gloria, Gloria Rhodes. I'm sure you don't remember me, but I surely

remember you. I overheard the nurses speaking about you, and I asked what

room you were in and if you could have a visitor. I told them it was

extremely important, and it is. This may be the last and only chance I'll ever

have to thank you."

With that, I wonder if this woman is senile and has mistaken me for

someone else, but I haven't the heart to burst her bubble and ruin her long

awaited, wish, so I let her go on. "Mr. McGiness," she continues, and instills

a slight shock in me at the acknowledgment that she knows my last name as well. Maybe she heard it from the nurses, who knows? She goes on, "I want to sincerely thank you from the bottom of my heart. Mr. Rhodes has unfortunately passed away, but about 3 weeks ago after being diagnosed with coronary artery disease we opted for bypass surgery. I was absolutely devastated, scared and overwhelmed for him, and it was you who took it upon yourself to comfort me." I try so desperately to recall the couple, but in the span of 3 weeks I've seen hundreds of patients. I fail to connect the dots on this one, but I offer a warm smile as she continues.

"I'm so thankful," she goes on, "that the anesthesiologist we got that day was you. You answered our questions with a care that put me at ease, eventually," she smiles as she jokes. "Through the kindness, and through the compassion that you extended to me that day, you made such a personal connection with me that, you may very well have saved the both of us, Mr. Rhodes and I," she reveals in a comforting, grandmotherly voice. Again, compassion is a theme introduced to me, one that's been disclosed to me in so many different lights as of late, and it begins to take a very permanent hold upon my psyche.

I quickly reflect on her words. This simply was all just procedure to me before; part of the job. I never knew I had this kind of impact on my patients. I never would have thought that they looked to me, for compassion. I just figured it was instruction, instruction they expected, and I gave it to them because I had to. It was my job. However, the deeper I delve into this reflection, I guess I can understand where she's coming from. We as anesthesiologists do play an integral role in keeping patients alive, and asleep, during surgery, no matter how long it may take. That's a tremendous amount of responsibility and risk, and those thoughts can understandably weigh heavily on the patients we encounter, and their loved ones. On a daily basis I am with these patients and their families, and at their most stressful moments.

I have the opportunity to offer these people confidence and comfort, and compassion, and suddenly, I'm thankful for that.

"Well anyway son," she says, interrupting the intimate vision I had produced in my contemplation, "I know you must be tired, and probably hungry," she peeps out shakily, laughing at the notion. "Thank you so much," she says. Placing my hand on top of the cool, clammy piece of bony flesh that is her hand, I offer, "Don't thank me, I was just doing my job. I actually want to thank you ma'am." "Gloria," she cuts in with a smile. Matching her smile, I go on, "Gloria, thank you. This is the most rewarding part of my job; not the money, not the challenge, not the benefits. I'm so grateful that I get the opportunity to offer compassion to so many people, and to comfort them when they need it most. Hearing about it makes my day." She slips her hand out from under mine, and begins toward me slowly, arms outstretched. "Thanks again," she says as we embrace. "You're very welcome," I assure her, "and thank you. You have a great day now okay?" "I sure will, now that I've talked to you," she promises with a gentle smile. The nurse flashes me a smile and then places a shoulder on Mrs. Rhodes, "okay Mrs. Rhodes, right this way." As they make their way out of the room, I get lost again, in thought.

Wrapped up in the midst of her story, I realize that I actually do love my job, possibly enhanced in the wake of this week's events and being inspired to become more aware, appreciative, and more compassionate. It's crystal clear to me now that one of the most rewarding experiences I can have is to have someone remember being comforted and placed at ease by the care that I provided. Surgery is very scary to many patients; to most patients. Reflecting further, medicine is exciting, as well as challenging no doubt. I get to use my technical skills to perform procedures, intellectual skills to problem solve, but I also have to use personal skills to help patients get through the anxiety of surgery, anesthesia and sometimes the pain afterward. Compassion is a very valuable component of the whole process. I see that now, and I'm not sure how I missed that before. Perhaps, not perhaps, I just wasn't looking. Compassion; thanks to it I now have a renewed passion for what I do, and, for life.

Just then the hospital phone calls out in an irritating, rattling chime. When I pick it up, I hear my wife on the other end, "Honey?" "Yes babe, it's me," I reply. "Oh, how are you?" she inquires. "I'm actually okay," I say. "I should be getting out of here pretty soon. How are you guys? How's Elli?" After a brief pause, she responds in an excited voice, "We're great. We were getting ready to come see you," "baby," I cut her off, "I just want to say I'm sorry, for the way," "Seth," it's her turn to cut me off, "we have a lot going on right now. You don't have to apologize okay? I know it's been a little rough lately with everything, the whole transition, but I love you, and that's all that matters."

Her statement has offered me a gentle solace, and I enjoy it with a pause of realization. "I love you too, so much," I assure her. "Okay Seth, so here's what's going on," she validates, in an even more excited tone than before. "We were getting ready to come visit you, and, well," she pauses in suspense. "Well?" I coax, aggressively. "My water broke!" she relays in elation. My heart suddenly pumps into maximum overdrive. "Oh my gosh," I burst, "that's fantastic. Well, I guess we will see each other soon," I joke. "We're on our way now," she informs me. "Rosie is driving." "Well once I get released I'm going to run home and grab some stuff for all of us, and I'll hurry right back okay?" I negotiate. "Sounds good sweetie," she chimes back emphatically, "see you soon! I love you." "I love you too hun, and I'll get there as soon as I can." "Okay bye," she fires back, and hangs up.

At this moment, I realize I am caught in a strange balance of exhilaration, and heartbreak. I'm so ecstatic at the thought of seeing my son in a very short time, but overhanging above this thought looms one consisting of the possibility that I may be told in the next 24 hours that I could have a terminal illness. That thought alone invokes so many different emotions, and for the first time, I have fallen all of the sudden on the receiving end of needing compassion.

"Seth," I hear another nurse call, "time to go. Dr. Adams wants to follow up with you on Sunday. In the meantime, give us a call immediately if you experience any abnormalities, weakness, loss of coordination, anything. Oh, and don't forget to schedule your appointment with the secretary on the way out; Sunday." "Sounds good," I reply, trying to gather my thoughts. "Is there anything else I can do for you Dr.?" she asks generously. "No, I should be fine, thank you," I verify. She closes the door behind her, allowing me the privacy to prepare myself to leave.

In the last few days, I've undergone such a radical, and positive transformation. It's helped me look at life in a whole new light, and as concerned as I am about the results, at the moment that concern is greatly outweighed by the wonderful sense of gratitude and joy I'm experiencing at the soon to be birth of my second child, my son. After changing, I make my way to the lobby to schedule my appointment; Sunday it is, 10:00 a.m. Outside I notice we have another day of summer bliss; this time though, even in the trenches of the waiting game for my results, the sun seems to shine a little brighter. The flowers, the flowers seem to radiate a stronger scent. This time when I say it, life is good, and I mean it.

In my excitement I get in the car with the pace of a thief trying to avert the authorities, and speed out of the parking lot. The good thing is, we don't live too far, so I'll drive the speed limit, well at least I'll try to. I turn on the music and head up the street towards our neighborhood. It's such a peaceful day; not many cars on the road, conveniently. As I smoothly make my way along the winding road, it's almost as if the stars were aligned just right and some higher power has parted the possible sea of traffic that has been known to frequent our back roads, especially on a beautiful Saturday afternoon. Instantly, a growing screech of burning rubber screams an anthem of violent turbulence in my nearest vicinity, but I can't make out exactly where it's coming from.

All of the sudden I see a bright spark of brilliant light appear immediately in between my eyes, and at the same instant, I feel the material of my car squeezing in around me, crushing my face, stabbing at my ribs and everything beneath, and slapping me in and out of consciousness as I feel my car tumble about the road as if controlled by a giant toddler, until finally I'm upside down hanging halfway out of the driver's side window, and barely able to breath under the weight of my smashed front end and driver's side door. One thought seizes my mind; I guess that's what seatbelts are for huh? In the hazy, blurred aftermath of the scene, I am right side up and it's impossible to make out what has just occurred. I can see a semi-truck directly across from my vehicle in the opposite embankment.

The most intense sensation of nausea has decided that it would inflict a horrid amount of putrid bile and the remains of some of the hospital food that I've had in the last few hours up through my throat and introduce it to my pallet and the rest of the world. I choke on it a little, and try to tilt my already disfigured neck even more, in attempts to try and expel the tail end components of my last hurl, and also to open up more of an airway, but I can't move, so I forcefully spew out what I can. I hear people screaming, car doors opening and closing, and the sound of voices coming my way. I see a puddle of my own blood forming a purplish pool around my head. Ironically, the sun that befriended my senses moments before has decided on emitting its brilliance directly into my eyes, making anything visible almost impossible to my sight.

Just then a man approaches, leans over me, and blots out some of the sun. I can barely make him out, just the outline of him. The rest of him appears a dark, shadowy coloration. Then, as he leans in further, I can scarcely make out his face. His features remind me of some of the Native American photographs I've seen here and there. Oddly, his eyes appear ablaze and a sort of steam or smoke with a very, very intense smell seems to be emanating from his body. As the smoke leaves his body it fills my senses with a euphoric sense of weightlessness. I've never smelled anything like it. He reaches out and places a palm on my forehead.

I instantly feel as though some magnetic force is beginning to pull my, well, to pull me out of my body, as I start to see myself and the scene below, and then it forcefully thrusts me back into my body, and I'm right side up once more. I must be dying. My senses seem to have abandoned me, and I don't feel my body. Actually, one sense, my sense of smell, is the only sense which, amazingly, seems to be overly functional at the moment. As this stranger leans in even closer, I can't help but be overwhelmed by the fierce sent of that something I've smelled since seeing his presence; something herbal. I can't put a finger on it; it's such a unique smell, and for some reason, it's about the only thing I'm coherent to at the moment. "It will be okay," he finally says. "Seth, focus on the light. Focus on the light," he repeats. Other pedestrians begin to approach and form a huddle around me. In the distance I can hear someone of the phone with 911. Suddenly a bright light is the center of my focal point, and everything else around it is a dull, spiraling darkness. It looks like the end of a tunnel, far away, but drawing nearer, very quickly. As it does, it's light burns bolder, and a warmth overtakes whatever still exists of me. There's no other thoughts at the moment, except for what awaits me on the other side. In the next moment, it envelops me completely.

CHAPTER 8

*T*here's nothing. I'm here, somewhere, but there's nothing. I mean, there's me, but it's dark and I don't hear anything. Thump; something clangs dully in the distance. Where is this? What is this? Beep, beep, beep... a consistent, steady beeping is generated from somewhere off in the distance. I hear a muffled voice, but can't quite make out what is being said. Suddenly a burst of pain shoots through, my body. My Body? I instantly become aware of aches and pains all over. Wait a second, am I, alive? A simple concept presents itself, one that hadn't occurred to me in the minutes before, wallowing in this darkness; my eyes. I attempt to open them. The lids are painfully heavy, and I contort forcefully to produce a small slit of an opening in both eyes.

Through the barely opened squint of my eyes, I see a figure in the distance, crouched on an uncomfortable looking nook of a bed formed in the wall by a window. It's a woman, sleeping. I scan the room for more, and it becomes eerily evident that it's the same room I had seen in a vision, just yesterday; a hospital room. Over to the left, I hear clanking reminiscent to the sounds in the darkness, and I see a nurse, turned around fumbling with some things. She stops, and slowly peaks over at me, maybe with the sensation that she had been being watched, and says with a smile, "Mr. Byers, welcome back." Mr. Byers? Who's Mr. Byers?

I hear stirring and heavy breathing turn into a breathy sigh from the direction of the bed, and look over to see her. The woman on the bed is now peering over at me, her body still turned in toward the wall. "Seth?" she questions as she slowly rolls over. "Seth!" she repeats at the top of her lungs, and jumps up to make her way toward me. "Oh my gosh Seth, oh my gosh," she says with tears rolling down her eyes. As she reaches me, a terror makes its way through my body and forces my eyes to widen into an alarmed goggle. It's her, the woman from my dream; the same hair, bleach blonde, messy with unsettled sleep, and the same makeup, smeared in a similar fashion across an overdosed looking face. As she embraces me I get a trace of cigarettes and morning breath.

"Sharon, we need to take his vitals and make sure everything is in line for his recovery," the nurse begins, as she makes her way toward us. Prying this woman, Sharon I guess, off of me, she says, "if I can have you wait in the waiting room, just for a moment, we'll come and get you when he's ready." She, Sharon, steps back sniffling. Looking at her I notice she's sickly looking. It's as if the muscles, what little she has, are gripping for dear life to the bones, and her skin has been messily draped on the surface. Her arms, riddled with track marks, produce very prominent bones. She, Sharon, finally manages to shakily spit out, "I told you I'd see you again. I told you that every night, and every night, I said I'd see you in the morning." With a smile, she turns slowly and makes way for her things, looking back at me here and there. She grabs a purse and jacket on the ground near where she was resting. She flashes one last look, and silently exits the room.

As I try to move a little, it becomes apparent that I have some sort of brace around my neck, and my wrists are strapped to the railings of the hospital bed. Surprisingly, my legs are free, and I attempt to bend them a little, and succeed, although it is a very daunting task. As the nurse reaches me, I see a few others enter the room. "Seth, do you know what year it is hun?" she begins. With more important questions looming in my mind, I slip out a, "where's my wife?" The voice I have produced is not my own. Actually, it's very high pitched, like a child's. I clear my throat, and attempt a follow up question, "my daughter?" This time, my voice cracks a little and is somewhat deeper, but still the voice of someone much younger than myself. I notice the nurse share a puzzled look with another nurse standing nearby, and she attempts the question one more time. "Do you know what year it is?" "2012," I answer. With that response she tucks her lips inward, and frowns a little.

"It's 2014 Seth," she instructs. "It's okay, you're still a little out of it." "Do you know where we are, Seth?" "The hospital," I say, evidently missing the intention of the question as the staff composes a symphony of quiet laughs. She replies with a smile, "I guess I had that one coming. I meant, do know what city you're in?" "Portland," I offer. "I'm from Seattle originally though." This time she looks unsatisfied, and a little uneasy. "Seth," she starts in, "this is Brooklyn, and you're from Philadelphia originally sweetie." In my dazed confusion, I actually become a little frustrated. "Vitals look normal," I hear someone call out from somewhere else in the room.

Another nurse, a male, begins removing the straps around my wrists. "What were these for?" I inquire in the unusual, unfamiliar voice. I sound like a kid. Well, a kid to me; maybe in his twenties. "You had some serious narcotics in your system when we got you," he informs me. "We needed to flush them, immediately. Notice the IVs? We couldn't take any chances. Some patients wake up and pull them out. You just never know. Weird stuff can happen." He nabs the straps and walks away. A doctor comes in and looks me over briefly. As he investigates, I shuffle in the bed a little, and my body seems a lot, smaller. I look at my arms and legs and am jolted with fright in the fact that my limbs have shortened considerably. This isn't my body. Well, obviously it is, but not the one I remember. Plus, I've got to be about a hundred pounds lighter. I'm 6'4", and a healthy 260 pounds; well, I was. I'm not sure what's going on; scary.

"Seth," he begins, looking at me with a slight concern, "we're going to runs some tests, draw some blood for laboratory work, and I want to do a physical exam and some reflective tests. Then you need to rest." "Can somebody tell me what's going on?" I ask in my delirium. "Absolutely Seth," he confirms, "I was actually planning on it. You've been in a coma for about a week. Thankfully, your girlfriend, Sharon, called 911 in time. Had it been any later, you might not be sitting here right now. You overdosed on heroin and had taken a pretty devastating fall off of an upper level balcony at the apartments you two were at. I think it was a party. Anyway, that's where the medics found you.

When you came in you were unresponsive; unconscious. Apparently there was a lot of mixing of drugs going on, because we found other drugs in addition to the large quantities of narcotics in your system. You had some sort of interaction, which caused you to stop breathing. That's when you fell. Adequate oxygen is vital for brain function Seth, and when oxygen levels are significantly low for four minutes or longer, brain cells begin to die, and after five minutes, permanent anoxic brain injury can occur. You were out cold for about ten minutes before the paramedics arrived. At least that's what was reported to them.

Anoxic brain injury, or hypoxic-anoxic injury, is a serious, life-threatening injury. It can cause cognitive problems and disabilities to the victim. Some HAI injuries are due to a partial lack of oxygen, like yours. Others, are due to a complete lack of oxygen. The greater the loss of oxygen, the more widespread and serious the injury will ultimately be. You're very fortunate, it could have been a lot worse. If and when the person regains full consciousness, he or she may experience a wide-range of symptoms, which resemble the symptoms seen after head trauma. The extent and type of symptoms are dependent on the amount of brain tissue damage and part of the brain where the injury occurred. This is what we'll be checking on."

"You've got this all wrong," I stop him, still unable to come to grips with what I've heard. I have a family, and I need to get back home to them. They've made some sort of mistake. That's the only explanation, isn't it?

"I've got a wife, a pregnant wife, and a daughter. I'm from Seattle and just moved to Portland. What am I doing in Brooklyn?" Suddenly I get a vision of a party, and I remember the apartment, with its red lighting, underneath the cloud of a smoky drug cover; impossible. "Seth," he says, snapping me out of it, "it's normal to experience confusion and memory loss after a coma, especially if there's been any injury to the brain. We'll be testing for all of that. We'll do some scans. You may even need physical therapy depending on the outcome, but we'll get to that. In the meantime, try to rest up."

After some basic testing, they clear the room and tell me to rest. I'll get a crack at trying to eat a meal a little later, something soft and smooth; easy to get down. I'm informed I can have visitors, and then the room is empty. As I lay in anticipation, I try to sort through what I've heard and contemplate any possible scenarios that actually make sense.   Minutes later, I hear the rapping of a knuckle on the door, and look up to see a man standing in the doorway. He's an older man, maybe in his fifties or sixties, and he looks, sad. He wears a haggard look of many, many years of strain and hardship. He's wearing jeans and a red and blue plaid shirt. He shuffles his way over, trading off eye contact with the floor and I, as he draws near. He slides a chair over, and takes a seat. Looking up and into my eyes, he begins, "Seth, you probably don't remember me." He pauses briefly, and then goes on, "I'm your father."

Coming to the realization that this is some sort of dream or hallucination that I'm not waking up from, I start to conceptualize the possibility that what everyone here has been telling me is actually the truth. Then, a great sorrow and regret fills me from head to toe, as I entertain the notion that the life I had just, died in, wasn't really mine at all, and that the relationships I developed, the enlightenment that I gained, was all some sort of strange side effect or something of this coma. "We haven't spoken in years," he tells me. "You were very young, just a little boy. I heard of your accident from an old friend of mine. He told me you had just moved to Brooklyn with a niece of his that he talks to every now and then. I had just happened to call him the other day, and he told me what happened. This was about a week ago. I found out what hospital you were at and I came immediately.

When I gave you guys up and moved, I told him that if he could, to always watch after you guys. You had a brother. You were twins. I figured you guys would stay close and he would see you here and there, and if he did, to let me know how you were whenever I could get a hold of him. Well, he did, and over the years he told me about many things. He said that you two had moved in and out of foster homes, and that you had been going to Father Flanagan's Boys Home here and there. It wasn't ever what I imagined my relationship would be like with my children, but it was better than nothing. It gave me some sort of peace of mind, even though I was torn apart every single day of my life that I couldn't be with you two.

Your mother left us when you were 4 years old, and at that time, in Philadelphia, it was extremely hard for a single man with only a high school education to raise two children on his own, especially in the low income areas of Philly. It was very dangerous. We had it rough when you guys were very little; lived off of the government with barely enough to eat. We took up residence in some of the most scummy, dangerous ghettos in Philly; the heart of skid row. Eventually, it just became too much for your mother and she developed a catastrophic drug problem, and on your 4th birthday, she left us. I haven't heard from her since. You see, I had a plan for you two." He looks down and shuts his eyes tightly, trying to force the tears to reverse themselves and retreat back to where they had come, but to no avail. With a stream of tears running down his cheeks, he looks back up and continues. "From the moment you guys were born, I could tell you weren't like them."

He wipes his face free of the stream that has just passed, and goes on, with a sniffle, "Like I said, I had a plan for you two. I knew you guys would grow up and be something. I knew you were better than them, the inhabitants of the shabby taverns and cheap dive bars; the lowlife, alcoholics and itinerants of the dilapidated hotels and rundown apartments of Vine Street. Living just west of the Benjamin Franklin Bridge at that time, was a jungle like no other. I knew you didn't belong there. That's why I gave you up. I always knew you would be something, something special, but you couldn't be something special there. I hope you forgive me for giving you up, but more than that, I hope you will one day understand why." At his confession, I am slapped into a brief, sobered conduct, and an equally baffled state, as the next thing that immediately jumps into my mind is, Mickey. Mickey said those exact words to me.

"I told you that while you were in your coma," he reveals. "The nurses told me that if I talked to you, you could still hear me, and possibly even make sense of it. I figured it wouldn't hurt. At least maybe it could be floating around somewhere in your subconscious for you to, to pull up later. You know, maybe later it would come out somehow, I don't know.

I'm just thankful I have the chance to tell you now." He pauses, and then looks at me through entertained eyes and a crooked grin, "you're not a man of many words are you." I shuffle a bit, and begin to spit out parts of words, trying to formulate a comeback. He shakes his head no, and puts a hand on my arm, "it's just a joke," he says. "Don't worry about it. I could only imagine what you've been through and I know you're probably still not all here. They explained everything to me, about what happened, and some of the possible, side effects, but you don't worry about any of that okay? Don't you worry about talking either, I can do that. You just relax.

I just want you to realize something." He leans in, in an attempt to drive home his message, "you're still very young, and you have a lot of time to turn your life around. No, this obviously isn't what I ever imagined you'd amount to, and it won't be. It won't be! You can change everything. You can still grow up. Yes, grow up; you're in your twenties now, but you still have a lot of growing to do. You can go back to school, be a doctor; maybe an anesthesiologist or something. They make the big bucks you know? You can have a family, a son and a daughter. You can live way up in the hills somewhere, somewhere peaceful. It's up to you son, all up to you. Son; I hope I can call you that. I love you Seth. Think about what I said, and get some rest now, son." He gets up, and offers me a few light pats on the arm, then he heads out of the room.

Once again in my isolation, I think, this is all so strange, and overwhelming. I look up and jump a little in response to noticing the nurse, the one I saw when I woke up, back in the room and looking at me. "Hi Seth," she begins. "I'm Rosalina. Your meds are over there on the counter." "Rosie?" I blurt in response." "Well," she says, "I don't really go by Rosie, but I like it," she giggles. "You can call me Rosie if you'd like. I have some medication for you to take; something to ease the pain a little, something else for the inflammation. Here's some water." She hands me a small Dixie cup of water, and goes to grab the pills. "Take this," she says. "They should be small enough so that you don't have any issues getting them down. Make sure you get a lot of water down with them though. I was here when you got here Seth, and I've been assigned your nurse for most of your stay. I'll be monitoring you for the next couple of days okay? If you need anything, press this button." She points to a nurse call button on a pillow speaker with TV controls. I'll be back to check on you in a bit. Oh, and your girlfriend, Sharon, said she'd be back this evening. She had to go, take care of some things." She leaves the room and again, I'm alone.

For some time, at least it feels, I sit and contemplate my new, evidently my old, existence. I haven't been able to process much of it yet. Everything has been moving so fast since I, awoke. I try to close my eyes to relieve my senses a bit, and possibly to stir up any memories or connections I can draw to this life and what has happened. Maybe, maybe I'll wake up again. Maybe I won't. "Seth?" I hear a voice call. When I open my eyes I see a man standing in the doorway. He's a young man, late twenties, early thirties. He lifts his head slightly in an attempt to get a better view, "you sleeping?" he asks. He waits in the doorway for my response. "No," I finally reply. "Come in." It appears I'm a popular guy today. I haven't been left alone much at all since, since I woke up.

He sits down in the chair that the man who said he was my father sat it, at an angle facing away from the bed, a foot or two from where my head rested on the propped up pillows. He places a book on my lap, 'TOWARD A TRUE KINSHIP OF FAITHS, How the World's Religions Can Come Together, His Holiness, THE DALAI LAMA. "Hello Seth, My name is Travis" he begins. A very close friend of mine said he knew you. He met you, well he didn't really meet you, but, he saw you, and has been following you, for about a week now." Following me? How could he be following me if I've been in a coma? None of this makes any damn sense. I slide my hand over toward the call button, admittedly a little freaked out at the intention of his information. "Wait, wait, don't do that," he pleads. "Let me explain. I believe It's for your own benefit." I look deep into his eyes. I'm not sure if I trust enough in his plea, but at this point I have nothing to lose. I'm still not even sure who, I am.

"His name is Alo," he begins. "Alo is Hopi for spiritual guide. He's drawn to, beings, who come from the stars, and who have the ability to travel throughout the cosmos, and they are drawn to him as well." "What does that have to do with me?" I inquire, a little tired, frustrated, anxious; all of the above. "I'm getting to that," he assures. "You see Seth, you have, special abilities," he says, as he looks more intently into my eyes. "You're what we call, a stellar trader. You're of a rare group of beings. Your abilities allow you to consciously travel outside of your body, anywhere in the cosmos, especially during times of what we call, parallel consciousness; dreams, hallucinations, daydreams, even comas. If you can learn to harness this ability you could tap into it at will, but as of now, it takes the influence of these times of parallel consciousness for you to use it. You can also take on the form of any being your mind can create, and, travel to different periods in time and take on the lives of those that actually lived at some point in the past. Of course you only possess their bodies, but the persona is your own. That is exactly what you did about a week ago, when you went into your coma. Since the time period you traveled to was in the past, you were able to latch onto someone else's prior existence, but since you were born in this body, in this existence, your body will always revert back to this life, even if you, die, in the alternate one.

Because you were born on this planet, this existence will always take precedence over any other place in the cosmos your conscience can go. However, your conscience can only be in one place at any given time, which is why if this body remains alive, your conscience will always return to it. That's why when you were coming out of your coma, when you died basically, your conscience was pulled back into this body." In stunned silence, my only response is facial, as I contort my brows and look down, trying to validate somehow, his message. "Alo was informed of you and your abilities through, we could say, divine intervention, and he relayed this information on to me, for a very important reason. As I said before, Alo is a spiritual guide; he's a guide to star beings. Naturally, he was drawn to you because of your ability to travel the cosmos. So, you could say you too are a star being. Once he was informed of you, and felt your presence, he traveled to you in the time period you were in, and kept a watchful eye on you until that fateful event which, took your, well, took you out of that body. Apparently he also has the ability to consciously travel to different time periods and different places in the cosmos, which he conveniently left out to me until recently.

Here's the point. According to Alo, you experienced some special things while you were in that existence; some, enlightenment of some sort." As I look back up I notice he is smiling. "I may have had a little to do with that. For a few days now I've been talking to you, quite a bit, about, compassion. I tried to express the immense power that compassion has on all of existence, and this goes for anywhere in the cosmos. Alo believed that the message hit its mark, and that you were, you were a changed man. He's convinced, as well as am I, that due to this, awakening, you are ready for the next step, the next major undertaking of your existence. I truly believe that with your story, you can help multitudes of others; other beings, other worlds. I could use these valuable gifts where I'm going. Anyway Seth, we can talk more about this later." He rises to his feet and places a hand upon my shoulder. "Go ahead and get some rest, you're going to be here for a few days. I'll come back when they release you; goodnight." He turns and heads for the door, stopping just short but not turning around. "Oh, in the meantime, it wouldn't hurt to read the book." He leaves.

10974013R00081

Made in the USA
San Bernardino, CA
06 May 2014